Mary-Kate and Ashley

Sweet 16

Win a
$500
Shopping Spree!

Details on page 131.

Truth or Dare

By Emma Harrison

HarperEntertainment
An Imprint of HarperCollins*Publishers*

A PARACHUTE PRESS BOOK

A PARACHUTE PRESS BOOK

Parachute Publishing, L.L.C.
156 Fifth Avenue, Suite 302
New York, NY 10010

Published by
HarperEntertainment
An Imprint of HarperCollins*Publishers*
10 East 53rd Street, New York, NY 10022-5299

SWEET 16 books are created and produced by Parachute Press, L.L.C., in cooperation with Dualstar Publications, a division of Dualstar Entertainment Group, LLC, published by HarperEntertainment, an imprint of HarperCollins Publishers Inc.

ISBN 0-06-059523-X

HarperCollins®, ▪®, and HarperEntertainment™ are trademarks of HarperCollins Publishers Inc.

First printing: November 2004

Printed in the United States of America

Visit HarperEntertainment on the World Wide Web at
www.harpercollins.com

10 9 8 7 6 5 4 3 2 1

chapter one

"Listen up, class. I have a special project for you!" my social studies teacher, Ms. Hahn, announced on Monday morning, as she picked up a stack of papers from her desk.

My mouth dropped open in shock as everyone around me groaned. "A project?" I whispered across the aisle to my sister, Ashley.

"She's kidding," Ashley replied, her eyes even wider than mine. "She has to be kidding."

"She seems pretty dead serious to me," our friend Brittany Bowen pointed out.

I opened my notebook and sighed, slumping a little. It was only a few weeks until Christmas vacation. I had been expecting nothing but simple assignments and easy quizzes leading up to our break. That was how it had worked every other year. But a "special project"? That sounded like a major chore.

"Shh! You guys! Maybe it won't be that bad," Lauren Glazer said with that ever-peppy smile of hers.

I swear, Lauren could be happy in the middle of an earthquake.

"I think you're really going to like this one," Ms. Hahn said, walking along the front of the room and handing a few sheets to the first person in each row. I sat up straighter trying to catch a glimpse of the assignment as it was passed back.

"For the next few weeks, all of you will be going to college!" Ms. Hahn announced.

Suddenly my heart skipped in excitement. I glanced at Ashley. Going to college? That didn't sound like work, it sounded like fun! I grabbed the last two papers from John Kline and handed one back to Lauren. I couldn't stop grinning as I scanned the page.

ASSIGNMENT: WHAT'S COLLEGE LIFE REALLY LIKE?

"This is *so* cool," Ashley said, not even bothering to whisper.

"I know," I replied giddily. "Now I'm glad she wasn't kidding!"

"The University of California at Malibu has agreed to let all of you join their freshman class for

2

the next few weeks so that you may complete this assignment," Ms. Hahn said, pushing her glasses up on her nose. "Instead of your classes here, you'll be spending your days on campus. At this moment, you hold a list of potential projects. Each one of you will choose a specific aspect of college life to explore, then you'll write a report about your experiences. You must choose from this list, so think carefully. Make sure you pick something you're interested in. Or something you've always wanted to try."

"This is amazing," Lauren whispered. "Look! You can assistant-direct a college play at the student Performing Arts Center. I'm so doing that!"

"You can take a whole class in American cinema?" Brittany asked, running her finger down the list. "Do you think you get to just watch movies all the time? College is the best!"

Everyone was chatting excitedly around me as I quickly scanned the list. There had to be something cool for me to do, and I wanted to find it before someone else snatched it up.

Get a work-study job in the cafeteria, I read silently. No thanks. *Rush a sorority/fraternity*. Not my style. *Study human anatomy in a premed class*. No way, no how.

But then I found it. The absolute perfect assignment: *Work on the daily campus newspaper and have an article printed*.

3

My mind filled with visions of me dressed in a responsible but hip button-down shirt and pressed skirt, my hair pulled back, a pad and pencil poised in front of me as I scribbled notes for a hot story. I imagined the intense atmosphere of a daily college paper! And I would be right in there, asking the tough questions, getting the big scoop. I could be the next Katie Couric.

"What are you going to do?" I asked Ashley as Ms. Hahn started walking up the aisle to jot down our choices in her notebook.

"I'm taking a psychology class," Ashley replied. "It says they're going to assign a human-behavior project. You know how I love to find out what people are really thinking," she added with a sly smile. "What about you?"

"The newspaper thing, definitely," I answered.

"I knew it. That one was made for you," Ashley said.

Ms. Hahn wrote down our chosen assignments and moved around the classroom, taking notes until the bell rang. I could barely wait to get out of class and get started.

"Good luck, everyone!" Ms. Hahn called out as we bolted for the door.

"This has to be the greatest assignment ever in the history of assignments," I said over my shoulder to my friends.

"Totally," Ashley said. "University of California at Malibu, here we come!"

My stomach was a bundle of nerves as Mary-Kate drove our pink Mustang convertible along a palm-lined road on Tuesday afternoon. I had gone online the night before to find out everything we'd need to know about the university. A map was, of course, my first priority. Once we got to campus, I wanted to blend right in with the students, not look like a clueless high schooler who had no idea where I was going.

"Okay, as soon as you drive through the main gate, take your first left," I told Mary-Kate, looking up from the black-and-white grid of roads and buildings.

"I'm so glad you thought to print out that map," Mary-Kate said, glancing over at it when we stopped at a red light. "And that you highlighted the exact route we need to take once we're on campus," she teased.

Mary-Kate was always mocking me for being so organized, and I always teased her for being so all-over-the-place. But it was just sisterly fun.

"Hey, one of these days you're going to thank me for my organization obsession," I said. "You'll see."

Mary-Kate grinned as the light turned green.

"There it is!" she said, pointing at a huge iron gate in a pale stucco wall looming up on the right side of the road. The sign above the gate read: THE UNIVERSITY OF CALIFORNIA AT MALIBU.

My pulse raced with excitement. "This is it!" I said. "We're going to college!"

"Okay, I make a left as soon as I get through the gate." Mary-Kate repeated my instructions as she pulled the car onto campus.

She put on the blinker, started to make the left, and slammed on the brakes. My stomach lurched all the way into my throat, and I looked up from my handy map. Orange traffic cones blocked off the road, and about twenty yards away a huge machine was tearing up the pavement.

"What do we do now?" Mary-Kate asked.

She sounded as flustered as I felt. So much for my carefully thought-out plan. I held up the map and tried to find an alternate route, but all the roads and paths and one-way arrows were too confusing to figure out under pressure. "I don't know," I said. "This is the main road that goes all the way around campus."

"Okay, this is not good," Mary-Kate said, watching as a tall, broad-shouldered construction worker in an orange hat approached the car.

The man did not look happy. *Okay, Ashley, chill,* I told myself. *Just figure out where you need to go.*

6

"Ladies!" the worker shouted over the noise from the construction. "You're going to have to move along!"

I swallowed hard and attempted to smile at him. "Um . . . do you know how to get to Wells Hall?" I asked.

"Hey, I'm just working construction here today," the guy said with a shrug. "Ask a student or somebody. But for now you've got to move your vehicle so my cement truck can get through."

I glanced over my shoulder, and, sure enough, a huge truck with an impatient-looking woman at the wheel had pulled up right behind us. I looked at Mary-Kate and bit my lip.

"All right, we'll go," Mary-Kate said, quickly making a three-point turn to head back the way we had come. "What should I do, Ashley?"

I glanced around. There was a big sign with a list of buildings and arrows pointing in various directions, but none of the names sounded familiar. "Well, if you take a right, we'll be off campus again, so—"

"Left it is," Mary-Kate said, turning the wheel. Then she let out a small gasp as she looked around. "Wow! This place is amazing!"

I glanced up and instantly forgot all about the map. Huge green lawns on either side of the car were crisscrossed with walking paths and dotted

with palm trees. Stucco and brick buildings lined
the lawns, each more imposing than the last.
Students gathered in groups on the grass, notebooks open between them, talking, debating, and
laughing. A couple of guys zoomed by on skate-
boards, their backpacks loaded with books. I
could practically *smell* the knowledge in the air.

It was exactly as I had pictured it. Everyone
looked so self-assured and independent, it made
me feel excited and scared all at once.

"Uh-oh," Mary-Kate said, coming to a stop at a
T intersection. "Which way do I go?"

A horn honked behind us, zapping me back to
reality. I was so mesmerized, I forgot to pay attention to where we were going. Some navigator I
turned out to be.

"Uh . . ."

"Come on! Move it! I'm late for class!" the guy
in the Jeep behind us yelled.

I saw a parking lot just west of us on the map
and I made a snap decision. "Make a left!" I said.

"You sure?" Mary-Kate asked.

"Yes! Left!" I replied, cringing as the angry guy
leaned on his horn.

Mary-Kate turned the wheel and hit the gas. It
wasn't until she made the left and was zooming
ahead that I noticed the huge DO NOT ENTER sign.

"Uh . . . Mary-Kate?" I said, my heart sinking.

"What?" she asked.

Just then three girls walked out of a building and stepped right in front of our car. I let out a screech. Just in time Mary-Kate slammed on the brakes again and the girls screamed and jumped out of the way.

"What are you doing? This isn't a road!" one of the girls cried, glaring at us.

"What?" Mary-Kate said.

"That's what I was trying to tell you," I said, pressing my lips together.

We both looked through the windshield and flushed bright red. Up ahead students jammed the pedestrian path, rushing to classes or back to their dorms. I sank down in my seat, mortified. I couldn't believe it. I had actually told Mary-Kate to turn onto a walkway.

"Omigosh, I'm so sorry!" Mary-Kate called to the girls. "What do I do?" she asked me.

"Try learning to drive," one of girls said with a sneer before they all walked away.

"I'm turning around," Mary-Kate said.

"You can't. It's not wide enough," I replied. "You'll drive onto the grass."

"Well, then what?" Mary-Kate said as a professorial type walked by, staring us down.

"Just go," I told her, wanting nothing more than to disappear.

"But it's a walkway!" Mary-Kate reminded me.

"Look! There's a parking lot at the other end," I said, pointing as I sank even lower in my seat. "It'll take us five seconds to get there. Just . . . don't hit anybody."

She hit the gas, driving by stunned students who moved to the edges of the footpath to gape at us. A pair of professors were so involved in conversation, they didn't notice our car until it was almost on top of them.

"Mary-Kate! Look out!" I yelled.

"Oops!" Mary-Kate swerved and the professors spilled their coffees all over themselves in surprise.

"Hey! We drive on *streets* around here!" a guy in a UCM football jersey shouted.

By the time we finally pulled into a parking space, I was so far down in my seat that my knees were pressed into the underside of the dashboard.

Mary-Kate killed the engine, slumped down, and covered her eyes with her hands. "Welcome to college."

"Look at the bright side," I said shakily. "At least we found a parking space."

Mary-Kate glanced at me and sighed. "Good point. So, where are we?"

"That's the not-so-bright side," I said, biting my bottom lip. "I have no idea."

10

chapter two

"Okay, just try to look as if you know where you're going," I suggested as Mary-Kate and I headed down a busy campus sidewalk. I lifted my chin and searched for a landmark—something I might remember from my map, which I'd crammed into my bag so we wouldn't look too geeky.

"What street are we on?" Mary-Kate asked.

"I don't know. There was no sign at the corner," I replied. "But it has to be one of the main roads."

Cars zipped past us, headed from one side of the campus to the other. A pack of people at a bus stop trooped onto a red minibus marked CAMPUS TRANSPORT. Students strolled around and greeted friends. I noticed that most of them were dressed down—in jeans and sweatshirts—and that *all* of them looked as if they knew where they were going.

"Oh! The University Shop! I saw that on the map this morning!" Mary-Kate exclaimed suddenly, pointing at a low brick building. "I know where we are!"

Relief washed through me, but it was cut short when a couple walking nearby and holding hands chuckled at us. *So much for blending in.*

"Great! Now everyone knows we're newbies," I whispered to Mary-Kate.

"So what? At least we're not lost!" she replied, grabbing the map out of my bag. "Besides, no one cares. They're all too busy talking literature and chemistry and the ethics of . . . I don't know . . . East Asian pottery or something."

"Well, at least let's get off this sidewalk with that thing," I said, pulling Mary-Kate behind a row of bushes.

"See? Here's the University Shop and here's Wells Hall, where your class is," Mary-Kate said, pointing them out on the map. "You're only a block away. And the newspaper office is just down the street."

I let out a sigh of relief. At least my little walk-way detour hadn't gotten us hopelessly lost.

"Well, now that we know where we are and we have some time to kill, why don't we hit the shop?" I suggested. "We're supposed to be college students, right? That means we need some UCM gear."

"Sounds like a plan," Mary-Kate replied. My sister was always up for a little shopping.

We folded the map and headed for the front door of the store. A few people about our age stood outside the shop huddled around a thin newspaper.

"Look! That's the school paper—the *UCM Herald*," Mary-Kate whispered.

"I can't believe all the stuff he's getting away with," one of the guys said to his friends. "This prankster dude is a genius."

I glanced at Mary-Kate. We both ducked a little to see the headline on the front page. Sure enough, it read: *Prankster Strikes Again!*

"What's that about?" Mary-Kate asked.

"I don't know. But soon you'll be working on the paper and you'll find out," I replied.

Mary-Kate grinned. "I can't wait."

"I know, Lois Lane. But you can't be *too* early, or you'll look like a geek," I said, hooking my arm through hers. "Let's shop."

Together we headed into the campus store. The place was awash in red and white. Every wall was covered with UCM gear, souvenirs, and supplies— everything from notebooks and pencils to blankets, mugs, and license plate frames decorated with the University of California at Malibu emblem.

"This is so cool!" I whispered.

"Come on! The clothes are back here," Mary-Kate said, grabbing my arm.

She pulled me to the rear of the shop, which was packed with racks and racks of T-shirts, sweatshirts, jackets, and sweatpants. Mary-Kate picked up a gray heather tee with the word *Malibu* written across the front in red collegiate lettering.

"This would be perfect for gym class," she said, holding it up under her chin and checking her reflection in a mirror.

"It's totally you," I said. Then I looked around and grabbed a black hoodie with the letters *UCM* on the left side of the zipper. "How cute is this?"

"Too," Mary-Kate replied. "Ooh! I think we need hats, also." She pulled down a couple of tan baseball caps. "College students wear lots of hats."

"Yeah," I noticed. "Why is that?" I asked as we brought everything up to the register.

"I think it's because they don't shampoo as often as we do," Mary-Kate said. "They're too busy studying and partying."

"Ugh! Really?" I said, wrinkling my nose. "I am not giving up personal hygiene when I go to college."

"You might when you see the dorm showers," Mary-Kate joked.

I cringed as we dropped our new gear on the counter, happy that our experience-college project didn't include living in the dorms. I wouldn't mind holding on to my clean, private bathroom for another couple of years.

After Ashley headed off to her psych class, I paused outside the *Herald* office, my heart pounding, and smoothed down the front of my most responsible-looking jacket. After many, *many* wardrobe changes that morning, I had decided to wear a plain white T-shirt under a sleek black blazer with my best jeans. The look was very "no-nonsense reporter." It was important to make the right impression on the *Herald* editor. He was the only person on staff who knew I was in high school, and I wanted him to take me seriously.

Taking a deep breath, I opened the door to the office and stepped inside. All around me writers were tapping furiously at computer keyboards. Phones rang. The copier whirred. A fax machine to my right was so full, it was spitting out pages onto the floor.

"Jason! Jason! I have the head of campus security on line two!" a girl with frizzy hair called out, rushing by me.

"No! Don't put me on hold!" a frustrated-looking guy shouted into his phone. He glanced at the clock and rubbed his forehead. "This piece is due in an hour," he muttered more quietly. "How am I supposed to finish it if you won't give me a quote?"

"Wow," I said under my breath. It was everything I had imagined and more. When the frizzy-haired girl rushed by again, I stepped up to get her attention. "Excuse me!" I said. "Can you tell me where Andrew Finnerman is?"

"His office is back there," the girl replied, pointing toward the far end of the room. She was so distracted, she barely looked up from her notebook.

"Thanks," I replied.

"No problem," she said. "Jason!" she shouted again, and she rushed off once more.

I walked through the craziness, catching snippets of conversations as I went.

"No, they can't give the kid a car to play football here," some guy argued with another. "It's against the law."

"You think the prankster might be a *professor*? Do you have any evidence to support that theory?"

"You can't report it without three on-the-record sources. We're a newspaper, not a tabloid!"

These people definitely take their jobs seriously, I thought, a thrill of excitement skittering over my skin. I couldn't wait to get started.

The door marked EDITOR was ajar, so I rapped on it quickly and stepped inside. A tall guy with dark hair paced back and forth behind the desk, listening to someone on the phone. The sleeves of his shirt were pushed up to the elbows, and he was gnawing on the end of a pen. I immediately sensed that this guy was all business. He glanced up and waved me in.

"I know," he said into the phone. "I know the budget is low, but we have the big end-of-semester advertising push coming up."

I wasn't sure whether to sit or stand, but his conversation sounded important, so I turned my back to him to give him a little privacy. That was when I noticed that the wall was covered with plaques and framed photographs. I stepped closer to get a better look.

Andrew Finnerman, Award for Journalistic Excellence, I read silently. *Most Outstanding Public University Newspaper: The UCM Herald.*

Unreal! Not only was I working for a college paper, but an *award-winning* college paper.

"Dean Arnott, I've got someone in my office. I'll talk to the marketing department and get back to you," Andrew said behind me. I turned around. "Thanks. Bye." He sighed and looked at me as he hung up the phone. "I swear, all the dean cares about is ad revenue. I could bust open the biggest story of the year, and all he would ask me would be 'Are ad sales up?'"

I laughed nervously, and Andrew gestured to the chair in front of his desk.

"You must be my high school writer," he said, shuffling through some papers as I sat. He picked up a note and looked at me. "Mary-Kate Olsen?"

"Yes. That's me," I replied. "But, actually, would it be okay if we didn't tell anyone I was in high school? I want to be treated like any another reporter."

Andrew smiled, and his brown eyes sparkled. "I like your attitude, Olsen."

"Thanks," I said, beaming. "And I want you to know I'm really excited about working here."

"Good, because I have an important assignment for you," Andrew said. He opened a desk drawer and pulled out a stack of newspapers. "Meet the UCM prankster," he said, dropping the papers onto the desk in front of me. "Everyone at this school is dying to know who he or she is, and you're going to find out."

Me? Unmask the prankster? With a rush of excitement, I leafed through the headlines.

Prankster Steals Park Benches!

Mascot Is Latest Victim!

Green Eggs for Alumni Weekend: Prankster Still at Large!

"Wow," I said. "This guy sure gets around."

"I've had four of my best reporters on this story, and no one has been able to uncover the prankster's identity," Andrew said. "I'm thinking that you—as an outsider—might see something the rest of us have overlooked."

My enthusiasm hit a speed bump. "Four of your *best* reporters?" I asked with a gulp.

"Don't be intimidated," Andrew said, smiling. "This person is sure to mess up sooner or later. All you have to do is be there when he or she does. But I can team you up with another reporter if you'd like me to."

"You don't have to do that. I think I can handle it. But I'll let you know if I need any help," I said. I tried for a confident nod, even though I was a little uncertain. What were the chances I'd be there when the infamous prankster finally tripped up? Still, Andrew was sure about me. All I wanted to do was impress him—and kick major journalistic butt!

"Good," Andrew said, standing. "You can use the office whenever you want, and just grab whatever computer is free. Our home is your home."

"Thanks," I said, standing as well. I was surprised he was ushering me out so quickly. "Is that all? Could you give me an orientation tour?"

"I would, but I'm insanely busy right now," Andrew said. "You'll find your way around. If you have any questions, just ask one of the other reporters. Everyone's really cool."

"Oh. Okay. Good," I said, trying not to sound as nervous as I felt. This guy was really throwing me right into the deep end, wasn't he?

"Uh, you might want to take those papers with you to start your research," Andrew suggested.

I flushed, embarrassed, and grabbed up the stack of newsprint. "Right. Of course."

"Your piece will be due next Thursday. We like to run big features on Mondays, so that will give me time to get it edited and laid out over the weekend," Andrew said, patting me firmly on the shoulder. "Everyone!" he shouted to the busy office, causing most of the people to pause and look up from their work. Suddenly dozens of eyes were on me. "This is a new reporter, Mary-Kate Olsen. She's taking on the prankster!"

I smiled and looked around expectantly, but no one even said hello. They just looked me over, then went back to their work. So much for the staff being "really cool."

"There you go," Andrew said to me. "No special treatment. Good luck, Olsen." Then he went back into his office and shut the door.

"Yeah, good luck on the prankster story," a harried-looking kid with blond curls told me as he breezed by. "You're gonna need it."

Gee, thanks, I thought. I tried not to let his words or the cold shoulder from the rest of the staff get to me. But as I headed out to find someplace to do my research, I just hoped I hadn't gotten in over my head.

chapter three

As soon as I stepped through the doors of Wells Hall Room 101, I wished Mary-Kate had come to class with me for moral support. I was definitely not in high school anymore. The lecture hall was huge—at least the size of a movie theater. Each row of seats was a level higher than the one in front of it, and they all faced a long white board down at the front of the auditorium. Hundreds of students packed the room, chatting, laughing, and going over their notes. The noise was louder than at any football game back at school.

Okay, look on the bright side, I told myself as I descended on shaky legs toward the front row. *At least there are so many people here, they won't notice the new girl.*

I slipped into a seat near the center of the first row and smiled at the tall, lanky African-American boy in the next chair. He flushed, smiled back, and buried his nose in his book. I was about to introduce myself anyway, thinking a little conversation would get my mind off my nervousness, when a heavyset man walked in through a door at the front of the room. All the students scurried to their seats as the door slammed shut behind the professor, and I sat up at attention, feeling a little sizzle of anticipation. My first college class was about to start!

At the last second someone slipped into the seat to my right. I took one look at him and almost fell out of my chair. My new neighbor was beyond cute. His light blond hair stuck out from under a red UCM baseball cap and he wore a gray roll-neck sweater that matched his eyes. He smiled quickly at me as he pulled out his notebook. Totally heart-stopping.

"Just made it," he said.

"Yeah," I replied, my pulse quickening. "Just."

Wow. I had expected lots of college boys to be good-looking, but this guy could have been a movie star.

"All right, everyone, last class we were talking about body language and how to read it," the professor said, running a hand over his bushy brown hair. He turned to the board, picked up a marker, and started writing. All around me pens and pencils scratched against notebooks.

Somehow I managed to tear my eyes away from Mr. Movie Star, and I yanked my notebook out of my bag. It was time to get to work.

"Can anyone tell me what percentage of communication is nonverbal?" the professor asked, his marker still squeaking against the white board.

I had barely opened my notebook when hundreds of hands shot up. Unbelievable. In my classes the teachers practically had to beg before anyone offered up an answer. This was so much better!

"Yes, you! In the red shirt," the professor said, pointing toward the center of the room.

You in the red shirt? I thought. The teacher didn't even know the students' names! But then, I realized, how could he? There were so many of them!

"Ninety-five percent?" the kid answered.

"Yes! Ninety-five percent!" the professor replied. "Now, let's talk specifics. . . ."

As the professor continued to lecture, I struggled to take down everything I possibly could, even though almost none of it made sense to me. I covered page after page of my notebook, my hand cramping and my palms sweating, just hoping I could sort it all out later. When the professor finally told us we could stop taking notes, I had written out ten pages, and my fingers seemed to be stuck in a permanent claw shape. Could a person get arthritis at the age of sixteen?

"Now I'd like to pair you up for your end-of-semester projects," the professor said.

I sat up a little straighter as I massaged sensation back into my writing hand. This was it—the whole reason I was here.

"You will be graded as usual, but whoever impresses me the most will be guaranteed an *A* for the semester, regardless of your past grades," he continued.

An enthusiastic murmur spread through the lecture hall. This was so amazing! Well, for the real students it was. If someone had gotten *C*s on papers all semester long, they could now wipe them out with just one good project.

"Okay, starting from the inside aisle and working out, break yourself up into pairs. If you're an odd person on the end, come see me. At the end of the class, one representative from each pair should come to me to record who you're working with," the professor instructed.

I looked down the aisle toward the center of the room, trying to count heads, knowing my partner would be either the beautiful-but-late boy to my right or the lanky-and-shy boy to my left.

Please let it be Mr. Movie Star. Please let it be Mr. Movie Star, I begged silently. Yes, I was here to study, but studying with him would be an added perk.

Fate wasn't working for me, though. The cute boy was paired with the girl to his right.

Oh, well. At least this way I won't be distracted by those amazing eyes while I'm trying to work, I thought. I turned and smiled at the shy boy to my left.

"Hi. I'm Ashley," I said. "Looks like we're partners."

"I'm James," he replied, flushing again and flashing a pair of deep dimples. "It's nice to meet you. I'll go register us with Professor Alexander."

As James walked up to the professor's desk and came back again, I saw the cute boy making some notes with his partner, a short, pretty girl who had her long dark hair pulled back in a braid.

He glanced over at us, then leaned forward. "You guys know what you're doing for your project yet?" the cute boy asked.

"Not exactly. We just met," I replied with a smile.

"But we haven't," he said, slinging his backpack onto one shoulder. "I'm Evan, and this is my friend Sloane."

"I'm Ashley, and this is James," I said.

"Oh, James and I go way back," Evan said.

"Yeah. We have half our classes together," James replied. "I can't get rid of the guy."

They all laughed at the joke. I was happy to see

that James was growing more comfortable around me.

"So, are you a freshman, too, Ashley?" Sloane asked, looking me over as we headed for the door.

"Uh . . . yeah," I said. I hated lying, but I didn't want special treatment from anyone. I wanted to fit in and to work just as hard as anyone else. If James knew I was in high school he might want to do most of the work—or worse—he might ask for a new, more qualified partner.

"Us, too," Evan said. "I haven't seen you around before, though."

"Well, I . . . I usually sit in the back of the room," I said, thinking quickly. "I just thought I'd try something different today."

We pushed through the doors, and Evan paused, smiling down at me. "Well, I'm glad you did," he said, causing a bunch of butterflies to dance through my stomach.

"Me, too," I said.

"Well, it was nice meeting you, but Evan and I have to get to work," Sloane said, slipping her arm through Evan's with a smile.

"See you around, Ashley. Later, James," Evan said. Then he allowed Sloane to drag him away.

"Are they together?" I asked James. I knew the question made it obvious that I liked Evan, but I had to know.

"Sloane and Evan? Nah," James said. "They're just friends. I think they knew each other in high school. So . . . when do you want to start brainstorming topic ideas?"

I wiped all thoughts of Evan from my mind and turned my full attention to James. I was psyched about getting to work on this project, and I was going to concentrate and do my best.

"How about right now?" I asked. "I mean, if you're not doing anything."

James's smile widened into a grin. "A workaholic. I like it," he said. "Come on. Let's hit the library."

After consulting the campus map, I decided that Cuppa Joe, the on-campus coffeehouse, might be a good place to do my prankster research before meeting up with Ashley to drive home. Plus I could soak up some of the college atmosphere to add a little detail to my paper for Ms. Hahn.

I cut across campus, approaching the small eatery from behind. Up ahead I saw a hand-painted sign over the back door.

STOCKROOM
CUPPA JOE ENTRANCE AROUND FRONT

A pickup truck was parked right in front of the door and as I got closer, a guy walked out of the stockroom, tossed a box into the back with at least a dozen others, and jumped into the driver's seat. Then he hit the gas hard and peeled out.

My heart hit my throat. *What a jerk,* I thought. With so many people walking around this place, driving that way seemed dangerous. I glared after his truck as I headed around the building. A bumper sticker on the back read: UCM SQUASH.

Squash? I thought. *That's the sport that's kind of like tennis, right? I wonder if the other guys on the squash team know they have such a reckless teammate.*

Taking a deep breath, I pushed through the front door of Cuppa Joe. Bells tinkled overhead, and guitar music played at a low volume from speakers placed around the room. The place was cool and casual, and I instantly felt at home. Booths with brown vinyl seats lined the side windows and toward the back was a common area dotted with students who lounged on couches, pillows, and beanbag chairs. A girl with short pink hair stood behind the counter, snapping her gum and reading from a textbook.

"Can I help you?" she asked as I walked up.

"I'd like a latte, please," I replied, digging out my wallet.

"So, you're on the prankster story now, huh?"

Startled, I glanced over to find a tall girl with curly red hair, glasses, and a ton of freckles leaning into the counter.

"I'm Shelby," she said. "I'm the last reporter the prankster totally evaded. I saw you at the *Herald* office today."

"Oh, hi!" I said with a smile, happy to meet a fellow reporter. "I'm Mary-Kate."

"I know. Andrew announced it," Shelby said, slapping a dollar onto the counter and grabbing a bottle of water from the fridge nearby. "Want to sit? I'll tell you what I know. Which is basically nothing."

I laughed as we walked to a booth. Shelby seemed outgoing and friendly, unlike the rest of the *Herald* staff.

"This guy has some serious imagination," I said. "He painted one of the school's buses pink right before the basketball team was set to leave for a game. He switched all the school's janitors' uniforms with tuxedoes. He replaced the mascot's head with the head from a pig costume. . . ."

"My favorites were the green scrambled eggs at the alumni breakfast and the time he switched Dean Arnott's license plates with plates that read *Mr. Mojo*."

I had to slap a hand over my mouth to keep

from spitting my coffee all over her in surprise. I
hadn't read about that last one.

"Yeah, that was pretty good," I said once I was
able to swallow. I tried to look unimpressed. After
all, I was supposed to have been at school here
since September. I should have known about
every last one of the prankster's jokes.

"But I still can't figure out how he stole all the
benches from the green," Shelby said. "Those
things are made of steel!"

What's the green? I wondered. I suspected it
was like our quad back at school, but I wasn't
going to ask.

"Hey! Is anybody working here?" someone
asked loudly.

I glanced at the counter and saw that the line
was eight people long. The pink-haired girl was
gone, and everyone waiting was getting impatient.

"I ordered a decaf, and the girl went to the
stockroom and never came back," the woman at
the front of the line said.

Just then the stockroom door opened, and the
counter girl walked out, looking shaky and confused.

"Uh . . . I'm sorry, but it seems we're out of coffee," she announced.

Huh? I thought as the small restaurant filled
with groans.

"What do you mean you're out of coffee?" the irritated guy asked. "This is a coffeehouse, isn't it?"

"Yeah, but . . . well . . . you're not going to believe this, but all the coffee is gone," the girl said. "Somebody replaced it with—" She paused and snorted a laugh. "With iced-tea mix."

I looked at Shelby, eyes wide, and knew she was thinking what I was thinking.

"The prankster!" she said, jumping up and running to the stockroom.

I would have followed, but my mind was reeling. Was it possible? Could I have *seen* the prankster committing his latest prank? That guy behind the coffee house—the guy with the UCM squash sticker on his truck—had been loading it up from the stockroom. He must have been stealing the coffee! The prankster had been right in front of my eyes and I didn't even know it!

Why didn't I get a look at his face? I wondered, my heart pounding. But then I realized it didn't really matter. I now knew the prankster was a guy, *and* I knew he was on the squash team. Now all I had to do was investigate. I had only been on the story an hour, and already I had my first lead!

chapter four

"Hey, Shelby!" I said brightly, dropping into a chair at the *UCM Herald* office on Wednesday afternoon. I was still riding high on my first real college writing assignment.

"Hi, Mary-Kate," Shelby said, taking a sip of her coffee. She did a double take when she saw my expression. "You look like a person who has a lead on her story."

"I think I do," I whispered, rolling myself toward the computer in front of me and clicking on the Web browser.

"How? Did you notice something at Cuppa Joe that I didn't?" Shelby asked, her eyes sparkling with curiosity.

"Maybe," I said teasingly. "You'll just have to read my exposé to find out."

"I'm impressed," Shelby said. "Well, let me know if you need any help. Not that you seem to."

"Thanks," I said, trying hard not to beam too proudly. An actual college reporter was impressed with me. Sweet!

I opened the UCM athletics home page and clicked on *Men's Sports*. All I had to do was find a list of squash team members and start investigating them. One of them was at Cuppa Joe yesterday. I just needed to sniff him out. It was almost too easy.

"Okay, we've got baseball, basketball, fencing, football, lacrosse, soccer, swimming, tennis, track and field. . . ." My heart dropped slightly when I realized squash wasn't on the alphabetical list. "Where is it?" I whispered, sitting back hard in my chair. I picked up my pen and gnawed the end. I tried refreshing the page. I tried a few other links, but the squash team was nowhere to be found.

What am I missing here? I wondered. This was not good. Where was my solid lead?

"Hey, Olsen!" Andrew Finnerman strolled up to my desk. "How's the story coming?"

"Great!" I replied automatically, smiling what I hoped was a confident smile.

"She already has her first lead," Shelby put in.

"Really? Nice work! Can't wait to see what you dig up," Andrew said. "Actually, the whole campus can't wait."

I forced myself to keep smiling until Andrew walked off. *The whole campus*, I thought. *That's a lot of people.* I stared at the computer screen, willing the word *squash* to appear between *soccer* and *tennis.* Unfortunately, my magical powers seemed to be on the fritz.

"Well, I'm heading down to the athletic office for a way exciting interview with the assistant swim coach," Shelby said, gathering her things. "I'll catch you later."

The athletic office? I thought with a rush of excitement. Someone there would have to know where I could find info on the squash team.

"Hang on! I'll come too!" I said, jumping up.

"Your lead is at the athletic office?" Shelby asked, raising one eyebrow. "Interesting. . . ."

"I'm telling you nothing," I said with a smirk.

"That's cool. Let's go," Shelby replied.

I'm telling you nothing because I've got nothing to tell, I thought. *But I will soon . . . I hope.*

❀

"Do they actually think they can pass these off as mashed potatoes?" I asked James, picking up a forkful of white slop and watching it drip back onto my plate. It was late Wednesday afternoon, and James and I were brainstorming over an early dinner. If you could call it that.

"No one believes those are actually mashed potatoes," James replied. "That's why I stick to dinner rolls and French fries. Not the healthiest diet, but it's about all that you can actually eat around here."

I pushed my plate away and sighed. At the next table a group of guys chatted over their dinners of cereal and toast while some girls picked listlessly at their wilted salads. *No wonder college kids eat so much pizza,* I thought. Without student IDs, Mary-Kate and I had to eat in some of the pay-as-you go dining centers or spend a small fortune in the cooler cafés around campus.

"So, have we narrowed it down to sibling rivalry or the actual effects of birth order?" James was asking.

"I don't know. Neither one of them seems all that exciting," I said. Being a twin meant that both were common topics to me. While I tried to think of a new topic, my gaze went around the room. The couple at the table behind James started to kiss, sliding their chairs closer together. I couldn't help staring. Who made out like that in public?

"What?" James asked, rubbing his nose. "Do I have food on my face?"

"No. Sorry. I'm not staring at you," I said, blushing. "I'm staring *behind* you."

James tilted his head and casually turned around. As soon as he saw what the couple was doing, he faced forward again and dragged his chair closer to the table.

"Ugh! Don't they know we're trying to eat over here?" he joked, grinning. "Sheesh. Sometimes I think people in love just forget anyone else exists."

Suddenly I was hit with a brilliant idea. "That's it! James! You're a genius!"

"I am?" James said, looking surprised.

"Yes! Why don't we do a study on the dynamics of couples?" I suggested. "We can talk to a whole bunch of couples and find out how well they really know each other. Like you said, they act like no one else exists, but how well do they really know the person who makes up their whole universe?"

"Interesting," James said, nodding. "And we could even break it down—see if the guys know the girls better or if the girls know the guys better. And also how well they know each other's nonverbal signals—like what Professor Alexander talked about in class—body language, facial expressions . . ."

"I love it!" I said, pulling out my notebook. "This is a project I can get excited about."

"Me, too," James said. "Good idea, Ashley."

"Hey, it was *our* idea," I replied, making a few quick notes. "Okay, so we'll need a list of questions. And—"

"Check it out! It's our competition!" a deep voice exclaimed.

I looked up from my notebook to find Evan

and Sloane approaching our table together.

"Hi, guys!" I said, quickly covering my notes. Evan might be cute, but I wasn't letting him sneak a peek at our idea. James and I both had grades at stake on this project—even if mine was for a high school class. As Evan had said, we were the competition.

"Ooh! Is that your project?" Sloane asked, trying to see over my shoulder.

"Maybe, but you'll never know," I joked.

"You're tough," Evan said with a smile. "I like it."

I flushed at the compliment.

"Come on. What are you working on?" Sloane asked, trying to take a look at James's notebook now.

"Sloane, chill," Evan said. "No spying."

"Just having a little fun," Sloane said. "Besides, their thesis can't be half as good as ours."

"We'll see about that," James put in with a good-natured smile.

"Come on, Sloane, let's go," Evan said, tugging lightly on her shoulder. "We have work to do. Good luck, you guys."

"Thanks," James said.

"See you around," I called after them.

Evan paused and flashed his heart-stopping grin over one shoulder. "Yeah. I hope so," he said, looking meaningfully at me.

I couldn't believe it. Was he *flirting* with me? I

hoped so. Just looking at him made my heart bounce around like a Ping-Pong ball.

Get a grip, Ashley. You're here to work, I told myself, focusing on my notes again. But try as I might, I couldn't stop thinking about the way Evan had looked at me. Maybe I could squeeze in a little time with him while I was on campus. As long as it didn't get in the way of my work.

❀

"Okay, I'm going to head for the swim coach's office," Shelby said as we walked into the bright, airy athletic department lobby. "I'll see ya later."

"Good luck with your interview," I called after her.

Once Shelby was gone, I took a look around. Glass trophy cases lined each wall, packed with awards for everything from women's fencing to men's diving to cheerleading and field hockey. Framed photographs of all the current teams were displayed on the right wall, and I walked over to inspect them, hoping to find something about the squash team. But as I moved from picture to picture, my heart gradually fell lower and lower. Still no squash.

"May I help you?"

A girl not much older than I appeared from a side door and sat down at the lobby's reception desk. She folded her hands and smiled up at me.

"Yes. I'm looking for information on the squash team," I said, trying to sound as professional as possible.

The girl stared at me for a split second, and then, to my total horror, she cracked up laughing. "The squash team?" she said, hand over her mouth. "Who has a *squash* team?"

I turned red with embarrassment.

"Does anyone in this country even *play* squash? I thought it was, like, a British thing," the girl continued, gradually containing her laughter.

"But I saw this guy last night with a UCM squash sticker on his truck," I said uncertainly.

"Oh!" the girl exclaimed, grinning in amusement. "Right, *that*. *Squash* is the nickname for Sigma Kappa Zeta."

I looked at her blankly, and the girl stared back as if I was completely clueless. Which I was. I mean, she was actually speaking Greek.

"They're only the biggest fraternity on campus," the girl said. "Everyone knows that."

"Oh, right," I said, scoffing. "Sigma Kappa Zeta. Of course. Thanks for your time."

Then, feeling like the outsider I was, I turned and fled the office before the girl could start laughing at me again.

chapter five

"She laughed at you? That's so rude!" I said Wednesday evening after Mary-Kate told me her whole miserable story. After dinner James and I had made up flyers asking for volunteer couples for our project and now Mary-Kate was helping me hang them up around campus before we had to head home—our parents wanted us off campus by eight-thirty at night. To speed things up so we didn't blow curfew, Lauren and Brittany were helping as well, hitting the bulletin boards located outside each department office.

"Tell me about it," Mary-Kate said. "There's a lot you're just supposed to know around here."

"Yeah, like what not to eat in the cafeterias," I replied. "FYI, go for the toast or cereal or fruit. Nothing else."

"Thanks. I'll remember that," Mary-Kate said.

She held a flyer up to the lamppost in front of

her, and I used a stapler to attach the page to the wood. Half the post was already covered with colorful ads for everything from a guitar for sale to a plea for a used futon.

"So, how was your day?" Mary-Kate asked. "I can already tell you and James got a lot of work done."

"Yeah. I'm *so* excited about this project," I said as we moved on to the next lamppost. "I think it's going to be really interesting to see who knows their significant others better, guys or girls."

"Girls, totally," Mary-Kate said. "We have a much better eye for detail."

"Speaking of details, you have to meet this adorable guy, Evan, from my class," I said. "He has the most incredible smile. He gets this one little dimple just on the left side of his mouth. It is *so* cute."

"Wow," Mary-Kate said, holding up another flyer. "Someone has it bad."

"Not *that* bad," I protested. "I'm not here to flirt. I'm here to study."

"But a little flirting on the side wouldn't hurt," Mary-Kate pointed out.

I smirked. That was exactly what *I* was thinking! Just then the door to the library opened and out walked Evan himself, trailed by two other guys. I knew from the lurch in my stomach when

I saw him that Mary-Kate was right. I *did* have it bad.

"Hey! Ashley!" Evan called out, walking over. "What are you up to?"

"Just working on my project," I said, holding a hand up under one of my flyers.

Evan nodded thoughtfully. "Couples dynamics, huh?" he said. "Not a bad idea."

I flushed with happiness. I swear I was grinning so hard, my face was actually stretching.

"Hi, there! I'm Mary-Kate," my sister said suddenly, nudging me with an elbow.

"Oh! Sorry!" I said, feeling like I had just been knocked out of a trance. "Evan, this is my sister. Mary-Kate, this is Evan."

"Nice to meet you," Mary-Kate said, shooting me an approving glance.

"You, too," Evan replied. "And these are my friends Darnell and Stan—Stan's my big brother."

Darnell was tall and broad with dark skin and buzz-cut black hair. Stan was a bit taller than Evan with a square jaw, dark eyes, and shaggy brown hair. He didn't look much like Evan at all.

"You guys are brothers?" I asked.

Darnell laughed. "No, they're just fraternity brothers. We all are," he explained. "When you pledge a fraternity, an 'older brother' is assigned to you to kind of show you the ropes. Evan got stuck with Stan here as his big brother," he added, slapping Stan on the back. "Poor kid."

"Ha-ha," Stan said flatly. Then he looked me and Mary-Kate over. "So, what are you two, twins?"

My sister and I exchanged a look. "Yeah. We are," I said. *Obviously,* I added silently.

Darnell cracked up laughing, and Evan clapped Stan on the shoulder. "You'd better get to class before you make an even bigger idiot out of yourself, man."

"What? It was just a question," Stan protested.

"Yeah. Maybe you should try thinking before you speak," Darnell joked, leading Stan off. "Nice meeting you!" he called to us, walking backward.

"You, too!" I replied, grinning. Darnell seemed nice. Stan, on the other hand, seemed a little spacey and rude. I was almost relieved when he was gone, glad not to have those intense eyes studying me anymore.

"Oh, hey! There's an ad for the concert on Friday night," Evan said, reaching past me to lift the corner of one of my flyers.

"Oh. Oops. Did I cover that up?" I asked. "There was no free space left."

"It's cool. Everything gets covered up eventually," Evan said. "But there's a killer band playing. Do you think you'd maybe like to go?"

My heart thumped extra hard. Had Evan just asked me out? I glanced at Mary-Kate, who grinned back. Apparently he *had*.

"Uh . . . sure," I said, smiling. "Friday night sounds great." I knew James had an on-campus job at the bookstore on Friday nights, so we wouldn't be working on our project.

"Good. How about I meet you at the gym around eight?" Evan suggested.

"The gym?" I asked, confused.

"Yeah. That's where the weekly concerts are held," Evan said, narrowing his eyes. "You knew that, though, right?"

Oops. One more thing I was supposed to already know.

"Of course!" I said. "The weekly concerts at the gym. I'll be there at eight."

"Okay," Evan said, putting his hands in his pockets. "And who knows? Maybe James will have to interview you and me for your project soon." He winked.

I bit my bottom lip as I grinned. Evan was practically telling me he wanted us to be a couple! This was so amazing.

"Well, see you in class, Ashley," Evan said. "Nice meeting you, Mary-Kate."

"You, too," Mary-Kate said as he strolled off. Then she turned to me and grabbed my hands.

"You're going to have a college boyfriend!" she whispered in a high squeal.

"I know!" I said, giggling as my excitement bubbled over. "Thank you, Ms. Hahn!"

❀

The next day I found myself wandering along frat row. The letters above the doors of the houses were totally unrecognizable. I saw the occasional *Pi*, a letter I knew all too well from math class, but other than that, I was lost. What did the letters *sigma*, *kappa*, and *zeta* look like?

"Okay, that one only has two letters, so I can rule that out," I told myself, bypassing a big house with impressive columns. I paused at a four-story brick structure with a sagging front porch. Three letters clung to one of the awnings.

"Here goes nothing," I said, rolling my shoulders back.

I walked up to the door and tried the bell. No response. I used the knocker. Nothing. I knocked again, loud and long, and finally I heard some movement inside. The door opened and a scrawny, shirtless guy with a goatee stood before me, scratching the back of his head.

"What's up?" he asked.

"Oh . . . hi," I replied, a little surprised by the blunt treatment. "I'm looking for Sigma Kappa Zeta."

"Then you're in the wrong place," the guy said. "And the Sigmas are jerks, by the way." He slammed the door in my face.

"Nice guy," I said to myself.

Discouraged, I hit the sidewalk again and checked out the next house. This one also boasted three Greek letters, but with its white stucco walls and well-kept lawn, it was in much better shape. I rang the bell and hoped for the best.

The door opened almost immediately this time, and two girls stood there in matching white T-shirts.

"Hi! Welcome to Gamma Phi Beta!" one of the girls said with a huge grin.

"Are you here for rush?" the other asked.

"Oh. This is a sorority?" I asked.

"The best and the brightest on campus!" one of the girls trilled.

"Sorry. I'm in the wrong place," I said.

"When you're a Gamma Phi Beta girl, you're never in the wrong place!" the first girl announced happily. "Come on in and see what we're all about!"

In the background a bunch of girls started singing and clapping.

"Um . . . no thanks," I said. "But have fun!"

I turned and jogged down the walk before the girls could drag me inside. Back on the sidewalk,

I saw a couple of guys walking into a big blue house with white shutters. They wore matching red jackets that read SQUASH across the back.

My heart leapt. The "Squash" house! I had found it! I raced up the steps and knocked on the door. Immediately one of the guys answered.

"Hey," he said with a smile.

"Hi! This is Sigma Kappa Zeta, right?" I asked.

"You got it," the boy replied. "What can I do for you?"

"I'm doing a story for the *UCM Herald*," I told him. "I was wondering if I could ask you a couple of questions."

"Sure," the guy said, opening the door wider. "Come on in. I'm Eric."

"I'm Mary-Kate," I replied with a smile.

I stepped into the gleaming wood-paneled foyer and glanced around, relieved that I was finally getting somewhere. In a room to the right a bunch of guys were gathered around a big-screen television, playing some video game, shouting and laughing. To my left was a formal living room, the walls covered with photographs like class pictures of the brothers sitting in formation. A few guys were working in the formal room, dusting the furniture and polishing the frames. They all wore red T-shirts that read PLEDGE across the front.

"So, what's your story about?" the boy asked.

"Want to know about our big Christmas fund-raising dance?"

"Actually, I'm doing a piece on the campus prankster," I said, pulling out my reporter's notebook. "I think he might be a brother in your fraternity. Do you think I could—"

"Sorry. Can't help you," Eric said, his expression darkening.

"What?" I said, my face falling. "But I only have a couple of questions."

Eric was already opening the door again. He stepped toward me, forcing me to back out. "No brother of Sigma Kappa Zeta would ever be involved in something so destructive and childish," Eric said. "I'd appreciate it if you'd go."

"The prankster isn't in trouble," I said, desperate. "People just want to know who he is."

"Thanks for stopping by," Eric said coldly.

Once again the door was closed in my face.

"What is with the people around here?" I muttered to myself. Now I was even more certain than ever that the prankster belonged to Sigma Kappa Zeta. Eric had gotten me out of there the instant I told him what my story was about. He obviously had something to hide.

Still, there was nothing I could do right then, so I walked off, wondering what my next move should be. The door opened behind me, and my heart leapt as I whirled around again, expecting to see Eric. Instead I was greeted by a tall boy with brown hair and big brown eyes. He was wearing one of the red pledge T-shirts, and he looked nervous.

"Hey," he said, walking quickly by me. As he did, he pulled a folded note out of his pocket and dropped it at my feet. At the end of the walk he glanced back at me, then scurried away as fast as his long legs would take him.

Heart pounding with curiosity, I grabbed the note, walked to the corner, and opened it. I was practically salivating as I read the contents.

I know who the prankster is. Meet me at the Tombs. 9:00 P.M. Friday.

My hand shook with excitement. This guy was going to tell me who the prankster was! I was going to break this story wide open!

But *the Tombs*? That sounded freaky. Was there an old burial ground on campus or something? I folded the note and shoved it deep into the back pocket of my jeans, then headed toward the *Herald* office to review the campus map. I had to find out where the Tombs were, and I had to do it before Friday night. Andrew had entrusted me with breaking this story, and I was not about to let him down.

chapter six

"Okay, I'd like to state for the record that college is *not* easy," I said as I walked into Ashley's room on Thursday night. My sister was already in her pajamas, pulling down the covers on her bed. After a full afternoon of prankster research and looking over the student profiles of the Sigma Kappa Zeta members, I could have crashed right there with her.

"Tell me about it," Ashley said. "Between going to class, doing all the research, and interviewing couples, I am beyond wiped." She paused and looked at me over her shoulder as she slipped into bed. "The plus side is, our actual homework is going to seem like a piece of cake."

I groaned and flopped onto my back at the foot of her bed. "I haven't even *started* my actual homework. For some unknown reason I promised Ms. Barbour I'd write a piece for the school Web site about my experiences on campus. Am I insane?"

"That would be yes," Ashley joked, pulling her knees up under her chin. "How's the prankster story going, anyway?"

"Good and bad," I said, sitting up again. "I have a meeting with a source tomorrow night. He says he knows who the prankster is."

"That's great!" Ashley exclaimed.

"Yeah, except he gave me a meeting place and I can't figure out where it is," I said. "I've searched the campus map, but it must be some kind of nickname for something."

"So? Why don't you just ask someone at the paper?" Ashley suggested with a shrug.

"Because, what if it's someplace where everyone hangs out?" I said, feeling desperate. "Then they'll know I'm an imposter, my cover will be blown, and nobody will take me seriously."

"Okay, okay," Ashley said. "What's the meeting place? Maybe I've heard of it."

I pulled the note out of my jeans pocket and handed it to Ashley.

Her eyes instantly brightened and she smiled. "That's the name of the band Evan's taking me to see tomorrow night!" Ashley said, handing the note back to me. "The Black Tombs. And the concert starts at nine. That must be what he means. This is perfect. Mom and Dad told us we have to be together if we're going to be on campus after eight-thirty."

"But it says 'the Tombs,' not 'the *Black* Tombs,'" I said doubtfully.

"So? Maybe he was nervous when he wrote it and left out a word," Ashley suggested.

"That's true. He did have to write it really fast, and he did look kind of freaked," I said, thinking it over. Ashley was right. This concert had to be the place. "Thank you so much, Ash!" I said, giving her a quick hug. Maybe I wasn't going to miss my meeting after all.

❀

"This band is great!" I shouted over the music on Friday night. Evan and I were standing at the front of the darkened gym, so close to the stage I could read the logos on the guitarists' sneakers. "I'm so glad we got to be up front!"

"I know!" Evan replied, bending slightly to speak into my ear. "Best place to enjoy a concert."

I couldn't have agreed more. But for me it was more about the guy I was with than the place where I was standing. Evan looked incredible in a black T-shirt and jeans, his shaggy blond hair slightly mussed. Plus he was a total gentleman. When he had noticed that the guy next to me was dancing like a maniac and stepping on my feet, he moved between us so that he was taking the abuse instead of me. Plus he was a great dancer. Whenever he started to move to the punk rock beat, I had to concentrate to keep from blushing uncontrollably. But inside I was beyond giddy. There was nothing about Evan I didn't like.

"Excuse me! Excuse me! Coming through!"

I stepped aside as a group of giggling, squealing girls about my age wound their way through the crowd to the front. They all mashed themselves into a small space at center stage and started jumping up and down, screaming whenever the lead singer glanced their way. Total groupies.

Evan looked at me and rolled his eyes. "High schoolers," he said, sounding disgusted.

My face heated up faster than you can say "Uh-oh." Of course I felt the urge to stick up for the girls, considering I was a high schooler myself, but something stopped me. Maybe it was the irritated look on Evan's face. Did he really dislike high school kids that much? After all, it was only December of his freshman year. Six months ago he had been a high schooler himself!

"I don't know why they let them into these things. These concerts are supposed to be for UCM students only," Evan continued.

I felt my shoulders relax slightly. It wasn't that he didn't like high school students. He just thought that UCM concerts should be for UCM students. Which was fine. Except that that would have left me out as well as the screaming girls next to me.

I looked up at Evan's profile, a knot forming in my stomach. Part of me wanted to tell him that I was still in high school, for him to know who I really was. But I didn't want to blow my cover or Mary-Kate's. We had both decided we didn't want special treatment while we were here. If I told Evan, he might tell Sloane and James, and then where would I be? James could ask to switch partners, and my project would be down the tubes. I had to keep pretending I was in college.

Everyone applauded at the end of a song, and I joined in. Then a slow tune started up, and Evan slipped his hand into mine, sending warmth up my arm. I couldn't help smiling when I felt that, and Evan smiled back.

Suddenly I felt silly for worrying about my school status. I liked Evan, and Evan liked me. That was all that mattered.

I circled the perimeter of the gym for the fourth time, my eyes trained on the crowd. Somewhere in this room was my informant. All I had to do was find him.

Unfortunately, the conditions weren't exactly perfect for a search. The place was pitch-black except for the stage lights, which flashed and pulsed and shot stray beams around the room. At least a hundred people were packed onto the floor, dancing and singing along, but they all looked like shadows. I tried to pick out the tall guys, but it was too difficult to see their faces.

If he's here, why hasn't he *found* me? I wondered, sighing as a couple of guys brushed by me, heading for the back door. Another song ended, and everyone screamed and cheered.

"All right, this is our last song!" the lead singer called out. "Thank you, everyone, for coming out, and remember, we're the Black Tombs!"

The last song? I thought. This was not good. In five minutes the concert would be over and this place would empty out.

I headed for the back of the gym, where a bunch of tumbling mats had been stacked up. The tower was about six feet high. If I could make it to the top, I would be able to see the entire gym. Even better, everyone would be able to see me. If the informant was here, he would find me.

Grasping one of the mats above my head, I easily scaled the side of the tower. I crawled out on top of the pile and sat down, my legs dangling over the side. Now that I had a bird's-eye view of the concert, I could see that everyone seemed to be having a great time, including Ashley and

Evan, who were dancing together down front. I had been so busy looking for my Squash pledge, I had forgotten to even listen to the music.

I checked my watch. It was after ten. As the final song came to its crashing, cymbal-heavy end, my heart sank. My informant wasn't going to show. What was I supposed to do now?

Soon the lights went up and the crowd began to stream out the doors. I glanced from face to face to face, looking desperately for my informant. Finally, Ashley and Evan were among only a dozen or so people left in the gym.

"Hey!" Ashley called up to me. "What are you doing up there?"

"Not getting my story," I replied, disappointed. I turned and crawled down the side of the mat tower, jumping down the last couple of feet.

"He didn't show?" Ashley asked as she and Evan walked over.

"Nope," I said. "Guess I have to go to Plan B."

"What's Plan B?" Evan asked, looking from one of us to the other.

Ashley had agreed not to tell Evan about my newspaper assignment.

I sighed heavily. "I hate to admit it, but I have no idea."

chapter seven

"Hi! May I speak to John Francine?" I asked, talking into a desk phone at the *Herald* on Monday afternoon.

"This is John," the boy on the other end said.

"Hi, John. You're the UCM mascot, right?" I asked, pencil poised above my notepad.

"Yes, I am. Who's calling?"

"Oh, sorry. This is Mary-Kate Olsen. I'm a reporter for the *Herald*," I replied, flushing over my greeting. I was so intent on getting my story, I had forgotten to introduce myself.

"Oh, hi!" John said, warming up a bit. "Are you calling to interview me about my trampoline tumbling finale? I'm the first mascot in Malibu history to attempt a back tuck in the costume, you know."

"Really? That's . . . great," I said. I had no clue what he was talking about. "But actually I was calling to ask you about the campus prankster."

"Oh. I already told a reporter over there everything I know," he said, sounding disappointed.

"I understand. But I might have a few questions no one has asked you yet," I said hopefully. "Do you think we could meet?"

"Sure. Why not?" John said. "If it'll help you find this guy, I'm all for it. After what he did to me, I've got a few things I'd like to say to him."

"Great!" I said. "How about this afternoon?"

"I've got class until four-thirty and then a game tonight, but I've got a few minutes around five o'clock," John said. "You can meet me outside my dorm, though. I live in Crosby Hall. Room three-thirteen if you need to call up."

"Got it," I said, making a note. "I'll be there. Thanks, John."

"No problem. See ya," he said.

I hung up feeling more optimistic. I didn't have a *new* lead, but I was hoping that talking to the prankster's previous victims might bring up something that had been overlooked. All I had to do was ask the right questions.

The door to Andrew's office opened, and I saw him walking toward me. Quickly I pulled out the keyboard from under my desk and started typing. The last thing I wanted was for my new boss to catch me staring into space.

"Hey! Working hard?" Andrew asked, pulling

his backpack onto his shoulders. "Let's see what you've got so far."

Heart in my throat, I quickly clicked the word processing window closed.

"What's up?" Andrew asked.

"I'm kind of a perfectionist," I said sheepishly. "I'd rather you not see the piece until it's . . . you know . . . polished."

Andrew nodded and patted me on the back. "I admire your professionalism," he said. "I'll leave you to it!"

As he walked off, I slumped back in my seat, pulling my pad toward me. Five o'clock, Crosby Hall. All I could do was hope it would work out.

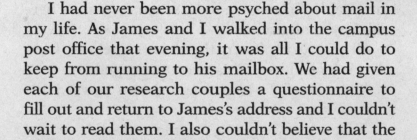

I had never been more psyched about mail in my life. As James and I walked into the campus post office that evening, it was all I could do to keep from running to his mailbox. We had given each of our research couples a questionnaire to fill out and return to James's address and I couldn't wait to read them. I also couldn't believe that the couples were willing to share what they really thought about each other.

"This is so exciting," James said as he twisted the combination lock on his box.

"I know. These things are going to be so juicy," I said with a grin. James shot me an amused look.

"And . . . interesting. On a totally academic level," I added quickly.

"Yeah, yeah," James said with a knowing grin.

"Come on, you know you're curious, too," I told him, crossing my arms over my chest.

"All right, I am," he admitted. "Especially about that one couple, Danielle and Theo. I mean, what do *those* two have in common?"

I was about to chime in when James opened his box and pulled out a stack of envelopes. A pack of soggy, disintegrating envelopes.

"Omigosh! What happened?" I gasped.

"I have no idea, but they're all ruined," James replied, peeling a couple of envelopes apart. The writing on the outside had run and was completely unreadable. "There are at least ten responses here and they're all useless."

All that work down the drain. Literally, from what it looked like. This was unacceptable.

"Come on," I said, tugging him toward the counter.

"Where are we going?" James asked.

"To find out why your mail looks like it went through a hurricane to get here," I replied.

"May I help you?" the smiling postal worker asked.

"Hi! We were just wondering if you had any idea how this might have happened," I said. I took the envelopes from James and dropped them onto the desk.

The woman grimaced and lifted the stack gingerly. "I don't know," she replied. "No one else has returned any mail in this condition."

"So there haven't been any floods or pipes breaking or anything?" James asked.

"No," the woman said. "I'm very sorry. Someone must have left one of the mailbags out in the rain last night. That's the only thing I can think of."

"Well, thanks," James said, turning away.

"That's it?" I asked under my breath. I don't usually have a temper, but I felt ready to explode. What were we going to do without the questionnaires? I had a feeling that "the post office ruined my homework" wasn't going to be an acceptable excuse at the college level.

"What can she do?" James asked me. "She can't magically make the responses readable."

I sighed. "I know. You're right. Sorry. I guess I'm just upset. How are we going to write our report without all that research?"

"We interviewed at least thirty couples," James said calmly. "There are still a lot more responses coming in. Don't worry about it."

The fact that James was taking this so well made me feel a lot better. "Okay. We should still have enough for a good test group, right?"

"Right," James said, grinning as he pushed open the door and held it for me.

"Why are you so happy?" I asked.

"Just glad to know you're such a perfectionist," he said. "We're going to ace this project, no problem."

Okay, this is a classroom building, not a dorm, I thought as I stood outside Crosby Hall that afternoon. *Didn't John Francine say he would be at his dorm?*

I glanced through the windows and saw a woman lecturing a classful of students, gesturing wildly as she pointed at her blackboard. I checked my watch. It was five minutes to five and John definitely wasn't outside. I had to find Room 313, and I had to do it soon.

Maybe he meant to meet him after class, I thought. *Just find the room.*

I walked to the end of the hall and up the stairs to the second floor, then paused. The stairs didn't go any higher. Two floors were all I had to work with. How could there be a Room 313 in a two-story building?

The door behind me opened, startling me half to death. I whirled around and came face-to-face with an older man carrying a tattered briefcase.

"Excuse me," I said, finding my voice. The man

sighed and looked up. "Sorry to bother you, but can you tell me where to find room three-thirteen?"

"There is no three-thirteen in this building," the man replied.

"But . . . someone told me to meet him at Crosby Hall, room three-thirteen," I said, checking my notebook again to be extra sure.

The man smirked below his mustache. "You're a freshman, aren't you."

I reddened at his insulting tone. "Yes, why?"

"This is Crosby *Annex*," he said snootily.

"There's more than one building named Crosby?" I asked, my heart sinking.

"Of course there is. They're named after Willhelm Crosby, the biggest benefactor in UCM history," the man said. "I don't know why the administration even bothers handing all of you that 'History of UCM' pamphlet at the beginning of the year. It's clearly a waste of money."

I couldn't believe it. I was in *the wrong building*. I had to find Crosby Hall, and I had about three minutes to do it. Leaving the obnoxious professor behind, I raced downstairs and out to the street, grabbing the first student I could find.

"Where's Crosby Hall? The dorm?" I asked.

"Six blocks up, make a left at the dining hall, then cut across the baseball diamond, and you're there," the kid replied.

"Thanks!" I shouted. And then I started to run. John Francine had said he only had a few minutes for me. It was going to take me at least that long to get there.

"Hey! Watch it!" a girl on a bike shouted as she nearly wiped out trying to avoid me.

"Sorry," I called behind me, still running.

I dodged a couple of marching-band members piling their stuff into a van, raced around a table of kids asking for signatures for some petition, and hooked a left at the dining hall. Up ahead I could see the backstop for the baseball diamond. Behind the fence was an L-shaped building at least ten stories high. Crosby Hall.

I turned on the speed and headed for the entrance—just as a crowd of kids began moseying inside with a couple of pizzas and six-packs of soda. They completely blocked my view of the door.

Come on . . . come on . . . I urged them silently as they took their time, joking and laughing. Finally I got a view of the door—and no view of John Francine. I decided to check his room, so I went inside, slid past the group of kids, and made a beeline for the elevators.

"Excuse me! Hey! You!"

I stopped in my tracks and turned to find a security guard glaring at me from his desk. What had I done?

"Key and ID, please," he said.

"What?" I asked, gasping for breath.

"Key and ID," he repeated.

I watched as the pizza crowd filed by the desk, showing their passkeys and ID cards to the security guard's female partner.

Oh, no! No, no, no. I have to get in here! I thought. "I . . . forgot my wallet?"

"Nice try," he said. "Unless you get someone who lives here to come down and sign you in, you're going to have to leave."

"Okay, but I know someone who lives here," I said. "John Francine."

"Great. You can call him from the security phone outside," the guard said.

Ready to scream, I raced outside and looked around. Attached to the wall of the building was a yellow box with a chipped sign that read SECURITY PHONE. I scanned the directions and dialed in 3-1-3-#.

The box rang loudly, and someone picked up.

"Hello?" a voice shouted from the speaker.

"John?" I shouted back.

"No. This is his roommate, Keith," the voice replied.

"Is John there?" I asked, crossing my fingers and holding my breath. This was my only chance so far at getting any new info on the prankster.

"No. Sorry," Keith said. "You just missed him."

chapter eight

"**E**van, this place is so cool!" I said as he led me from room to room in his fraternity house. We were both taking a break from studying and had decided to go out for mid-afternoon pizza, but Evan had offered to give me a tour of the Sigma Kappa Zeta house first. "Do you get to have your own bathroom?"

"Unfortunately, no," Evan said with a laugh. "But it's a lot less gross than the ones in the dorms. We have a service that comes in to clean twice a week."

"Nice. Maybe I'll live in a sorority when I—" I bit my tongue, realizing my near mistake. I had almost said, *"when I go to college."*

"Are you thinking about pledging?" Evan asked. "Because you definitely should. It was the best thing I ever did. This school is so huge, and belonging to a fraternity makes it feel smaller.

Like I have a place to go home to, you know? Plus I got really lucky. Right after I finished pledging in October, a spot opened up in the house, and I got to move in."

"Sounds great," I said, my pulse returning to normal. He hadn't noticed my slipup. We walked past the dining room. Inside were three long tables, and a bunch of guys were seated along them, working on an arts-and-crafts project. Hand cut snowflakes were strewn about along with tons of glitter and red and green paper.

"Holiday decorations?" I asked.

"Yeah. The pledges are in charge of making the stuff for our annual winter dance," Evan said, stepping back into the hall. "Actually, Ashley, I've been meaning to ask you," he said, looking at the floor and blushing. "Would you like to go with me to the dance?" he asked, the words coming out in a rush.

"I'd love to!" I replied, elated. A college dance! With an amazing guy!

"Great!" Evan said, brightening. "So, let's go get that pizza."

"Okay," I said, still beaming. "I should get my laptop and stuff from your room, though."

"Eh, just leave it," Evan said. "We can stop back here afterward, and then you don't have to lug it with you."

"Good idea," I said. My shoulders already ached from the laptop bag and my heavy backpack. Just as Evan and I got to the front door, Stan and Darnell walked in.

"Hey! Where are you guys off to?" Darnell asked.

"Getting some pizza," Evan replied.

"Do you want us to bring you back something?" I asked.

"Yeah. Get us a pie with everything," Stan said, patting his sizable stomach. "Make that two. I'm starving."

"So much for getting into shape by Christmas, huh, Stan?" Darnell joked, slapping his friend on the back.

I bit my lip to keep from laughing.

"Hey, the girl asked," Stan replied. "You know what? I like you," he added, looking me up and down. "She's way cooler than Giggle Fit, Ev."

"Giggle Fit?" I asked, raising my eyebrows.

"When I started pledging I used to bring my girlfriend around," Evan explained. "She was still in high school, and she was kind of a giggler."

"High school girls. Total dorks," Stan said.

Um . . . hello? I thought, my stomach churning. *Prejudiced much?*

"Anyway, I broke up with her right around then," Evan added with a shrug. "Gotta grow up sometime, right?"

"I never called her Giggle Fit," Darnell said, clearly noticing my offended expression. "For the record."

"So, let's get going. We both have to get back to our project partners soon," Evan said.

I nodded and followed him out, but there was an uncomfortable knot in the pit of my stomach.

"I can't believe they charge twenty dollars just to get into a basketball game," I muttered to myself as I waited outside the locker room door.

Apparently students with a college ID got in for free. Those of us lame enough to be pre-frosh were not so lucky. As important as this story was, I couldn't afford to waste all the money in my wallet.

The locker room door banged open, and out poured five cheerleaders, still in their red and white UCM uniforms. Seconds later fans started streaming out the general exit, talking and cheering. I rushed over to the cheerleaders before they could get lost in the crowd.

"Hi! Is John Francine still inside?" I asked.

"He'll be out in a minute," one of the girls answered.

I thanked her, then waited off to one side. I had to ask this guy a few questions before it was too late.

A few minutes later the double doors opened and not one but two mascots walked out. One wore a brown feathered costume with a red shirt and had an eagle head under his arm. The other wore a gray costume with a red shirt and an armadillo head under his arm. I froze. Which one was the UCM mascot? How had I never noticed which animal represented the school?

I had to think fast. Any second they were both going to walk right by me.

Okay, an armadillo I'd remember, but an eagle is much more forgettable, I told myself. *It has to be the eagle.*

Hoping my logic was logical, I rushed up to the sweaty, tired-looking eagle.

"Hi, are you John?" I asked.

"Yep, that's me," the guy said with a smile.

I was right! Total relief.

"I'm Mary-Kate Olsen. From the *Herald*," I said.

"Hey," he replied. "What can I do for you?"

"I just have a couple of questions," I said as the crowd streamed by us.

"Is this about the new halftime routine?" he asked. "If so, you should really be talking to Lorraine Marks. She choreographed the whole thing."

My brow furrowed. This guy really liked to push his routine. "No, this is about the campus prankster, remember?"

"The campus prankster?" His eyes went totally blank. My stomach clenched. *Oh, no. No!*

"You are John Francine, aren't you?" I asked, holding my breath.

"No, sorry. John Dunne," he replied. "Oh, man. I gotta catch my bus. Sorry."

John Dunne. How could they both have the same first name? How could I be that unlucky? All I could do was stand there as the eagle jogged over to a big red bus that read CAL STATE EAGLES on the side. I had stopped the wrong mascot. And now the armadillo was nowhere to be seen.

Tuesday evening I walked into the *Herald* office, exhausted and depressed. Trying to be a college reporter was definitely taking a lot out of me. I slumped into the chair next to Shelby's and sighed. All I wanted was one lead. Just one.

"Wow," Shelby said, leaning back. "That is the look of a person who has been duped by the prankster."

"I'm just tired," I told her, trying to sit up straight and look positive.

"Well, I don't know if this is going to help you at all, but Marta, the girl in charge of the mail, found this in the general inbox," Shelby said. She tossed a cream-colored envelope onto the desk in front of me and eyed me curiously.

My eyes widened, and my heart started to pound out of control. It was addressed to *Mary-Kate: the reporter on the prankster story.* And the handwriting looked just like the writing on the first note from my mystery informant—the guy who had never shown up at the concert.

"Secret admirer, or secret source?" Shelby asked.

"You ask too many questions," I joked, suddenly very awake.

"Hey, it's my job," Shelby replied with a shrug.

I smiled, ripped open the envelope with shaking hands, and spun in my chair to block the contents from Shelby.

> *Mary-Kate,*
> *You missed our first meeting. If you still want info, meet me at the Center tomorrow night. 8:00 P.M.*
> *The Pledge*

Yes! He was giving me another chance! But when I read the note again, my face fell. The Center? What was the Center? Why couldn't he pick a place I knew?

I thought about asking Shelby, but I was afraid the question might get her thinking. I'd have to remember to ask Ashley or Brittany or Lauren if one of them had heard of someplace referred to as the Center.

chapter nine

"**Y**ou ready for this?" James asked me on Tuesday as I flipped the switch on my laptop.

The machine whirred to life, and I smiled. "I'm actually psyched to get to work," I replied, glancing around the study-group room of the library. At each of the wide tables students pored over books and checked each other's notes. The intensity in the room sent tingles up my spine.

"Well, at least we have some clean responses," James said, pulling a new stack of mail from his bag. "We can write the introduction from our interviews and research, then get to work on these questionnaires."

The laptop screen blinked to life, and I moved the little arrow around for a second, waiting for all my desktop icons to appear.

I waited. And waited. I saw my word-processing icon. My folders for all my regular schoolwork.

My Internet icon and my music program and my folder full of digital pictures. But where was my new *Psychology* folder?

My heart skipped a beat. Something was very wrong.

"What's up?" James asked.

"I could have sworn I created a desktop folder for the project." I quickly opened the main menu and scanned all the folders. There was no *Psychology* icon. "It was there yesterday," I said.

"Here. Let me try something," James said. He opened the search function and typed in *Psychology*. The computer searched all the drives and then a window popped up in the center of the screen with three words: *File Not Found*.

"Oh, no," James said. "All our research was on your computer. The transcripts from all our interviews. . . ."

I was starting to feel sick to my stomach. And then it hit me. My organizational obsession was about to pay off. Big-time.

"It's okay!" I said. "I backed everything up on disk."

James looked as relieved as I felt. "I should have known you were smart enough to do that," he said.

Smiling, I leaned down and opened the outside pocket on my laptop bag, sliding my hand inside. My heart skipped a beat. It was empty.

Okay. Don't panic. You probably just put them somewhere else, I told myself. I searched a side pocket thoroughly, then the one on the other side, then the one in the center. The bag was empty.

"What? What is it?" James asked.

"My disks," I said, my mouth dry. "They're gone."

"Do you remember taking them out?" James asked.

"No. I don't. I *know* I didn't." I dropped the bag back onto the floor and looked at James, unable to believe what I was about to say. "I think someone's been messing with my computer."

"What? Who would do that?" James asked.

"I have no idea," I replied, racking my brain. This wasn't happening. It couldn't be happening. All that work!

"Well . . . have you let it out of your sight at all?" James asked.

My stomach churned, and I pressed my lips together. "I . . . I left it in Evan's room at his fraternity house yesterday," I said slowly.

"Wait a minute. Evan deleted our files and stole your disks?" James said, his face going slack. "That doesn't sound like him."

"It wasn't him. It couldn't have been," I said. "He was with me the whole time. I took my backpack and my computer the second we got back from dinner."

"So, what then? Someone in his fraternity did it?" James said.

"I guess so. But who?" I asked. "Why would anyone in Evan's fraternity want to sabotage our psychology project?"

❀

I had it right this time. I knew I did. It was Wednesday evening, and I was standing outside the Performing Arts Center, waiting for my informant. After going over the campus map carefully, I had figured out that "the Center" was short for the Performing Arts Center. It had to be. My informant would be here any second now, and by this time tomorrow I would have my story.

Students and faculty walked in and out through the glass doors of the brightly lit building, and I checked them all out, looking for "the pledge." Of course, this time I was certain *he* would find *me*. I wore a bright white sweater and had placed myself right in the center of the stairs leading up to the main doors. No way could he miss me.

I took a deep breath. I was so excited to hear what the pledge had to say that I was bouncing up and down on the balls of my feet.

Calm down. Be professional, I told myself. This was a huge, important story. My first college article. I didn't want to look like an eager kid at a carnival.

It was a beautiful, warm night, and a lot of the students were carrying garment bags and boxes into the Center. I remembered that Lauren's project for Ms. Hahn was to assist the direction of a play. They were doing a musical, *The Wiz*. Was the performance tonight? Maybe my informant was going to see the show and wanted to meet me beforehand.

I checked my watch, and my pulse raced. It was five after eight. The pledge was already late. Not a good sign. But I was in the right place this time. Wasn't I?

"Mary-Kate!"

My heart leapt before I realized that it was a girl's voice that was calling my name. I looked up to find Lauren jogging toward me. She was wearing a black turtleneck with black pants, and her brown hair was pulled back in a tight bun.

"What are you doing here? Did you come to watch the dress rehearsal?" Lauren asked excitedly, giving me a quick hug.

"Dress rehearsal?" I asked blankly. My mind was kind of elsewhere.

"Tonight's our first full run-through," Lauren said. "It's going to be so awesome! You have to come see it if you can. Opening night is next week."

"I'd love to," I said, smiling at her giddiness. "How is your project going? Are you having fun?"

"Oh, the *most* fun," Lauren assured me. "Bob, the director? He gave me all this responsibility. I have to make sure everyone is ready in the wings before their scenes, and I'm overseeing the prop-man and the set director. Everyone is so professional. How's working on the *Herald*?"

"It's . . . great," I lied. I was starting to feel as if I wasn't worthy of working on a college newspaper. I couldn't even get in touch with a source who was practically throwing himself at me.

"Well, I should get inside," Lauren said, checking her watch. "We're starting in a few minutes. See you later!"

"Lauren, wait!" I called after her. Part of me didn't want to ask this question, but I had to. I had to know. "Do they call this place 'the Center'?"

Lauren blinked, confused. "Actually they call it the PAC—short for Performing Arts Center," she said. "I think they call the Student Center 'the Center,' though. We hang out there after rehearsals sometimes."

I saw my life flashing before my eyes. I was in the wrong place! *Again!* Lauren was watching me with a concerned expression, so I forced a smile.

"Thanks," I said. "Break a leg."

As soon as Lauren disappeared inside, I ran. I cut across College Avenue and skidded to a stop in front of the huge brick structure that housed a game room, a few fast-food restaurants, and a big atrium filled with tables. The Student Center. The huge clock on the front of the building told me it was 8:20. Could he possibly still be inside?

Crossing my fingers for luck, I jogged in and looked around the wide lobby. A couple of students lounged on the benches, but no one looked familiar. I ran downstairs and walked around the game room, checking aisle after aisle of arcade games and scanning the faces at the Ping-Pong and air hockey tables. He wasn't there. I trudged to the food court. The lines were long in front of the burger place, the pizza place, and the Chinese take-out counter, but the pledge wasn't there.

I had missed him again.

I sank into the nearest chair and put my head in my hands. What was I going to do now?

Okay, I could just go over to the Squash house and bang on the door, I thought. But I had no idea what the pledge's name was. Besides, he kept trying to meet me in secret, which clearly meant he didn't want the brothers to know he was talking to me. If I stormed into his fraternity house, he might deny he even knew me. Then where would I be?

Nowhere. Just like I was right now. My story was due the next day, and I had no new information for Andrew. Zip. *Nada.* The big zero. I had messed up my only lead. What was I going to do?

chapter ten

"So you're both graduating this spring, and you've been together since the second week of your freshman year?" I asked the couple sitting before me.

"Yep," Trent said, reaching out to hold Holly's hand. "And every day I love her more."

Holly blushed and smiled as James typed furiously into the computer. For the past two hours James and I had been conducting new interviews for our psych paper, and I found each couple more fascinating than the last. Maybe all our previous work had disappeared, but there was a bright side. I was meeting more and more cool people.

"Wow. So do you guys think you'll get engaged after graduation?" I asked.

Instantly Trent's hand jerked back, and Holly's smile disappeared.

"I didn't say anything about marriage," Trent said. "Did you say anything about marriage?" he asked Holly.

"Why are you freaking out?" Holly asked. "The girl just asked a question."

"Well, we're . . . we're only twenty-one," Trent stammered. "I mean, *engaged*? That's like nine . . . ten years off!"

"Nine or ten *years*?" Holly said, her mouth dropping open. "You never said that before!"

I watched the exchange, noting body language and tone of voice like a good psych student. Holly was completely shocked, and poor Trent looked like a cornered rabbit.

"Okay, you guys. Calm down," I said. "I didn't mean to start an argument."

"I have to go," Holly said, grabbing her messenger bag. "Good luck with your project, Ashley . . . James." She stormed out of the Student Center without a glance back.

"Guess I should go, too," Trent added, slinking after her.

"Thanks for your help!" I shouted.

"Well, that was interesting," James said, fighting a smile as he hit a few more keys on the keyboard.

"Yeah. Did you see the defensiveness there?" I asked. "That guy is not ready for a commitment."

"Definitely not," James said. He glanced up at the clock. "We'd better pack up. Class starts in ten minutes."

"Right," I said, closing my notebook and shoving it into my backpack. "I think we got some really good stuff today, don't you?"

"Absolutely," James said with a grin. "We just might pull this project off after all."

"Yeah. So what if we had to do twice the work?" I joked, picking up my computer and placing it in the bag. "It'll just be twice as good."

At that moment I really was feeling confident. The one good thing about studying people was that they were never short on interesting information.

Together we walked out the main door of the Student Center, but as soon as we hit the sidewalk, I stopped in my tracks. There, across the street, was Sloane—Evan's project partner—and she was tearing flyers down from utility poles. *Our* flyers.

"I don't believe it," I said. "Look."

James's eyes widened when he saw Sloane. He stalked across the street so fast, I could barely keep up.

"Sloane! What are you doing?" James asked.

Sloane's face went white. She looked at the crumpled mess of flyers in her hand. The evidence was right there.

"I . . . uh . . ." Sloane stammered.

"You were tearing down our flyers!" I said. "How could you do that?"

Before Sloane could answer, Evan walked out of the dining hall behind her. He grinned when he spotted us. "Hey, guys! Going to class?" he asked.

Sloane looked guiltily at Evan, then shoved the crumpled flyers into her pocket. Suddenly it all became clear. It wasn't Evan or any of his fraternity brothers who had messed with my computer. It was Sloane!

"Sloane, have you been trying to sabotage our project?" I asked point-blank.

"What?" Evan asked with a laugh. "You're kidding, right?"

"I don't know," I said. "Did she have access to your room on Monday night? The night we went out for pizza?"

Evan looked at Sloane. "Wasn't that the night you stopped by to borrow my chem textbook?" he asked.

Sloane swallowed hard. "Yeah, but I—"

"And the letters?" I asked. "Did you do something to the questionnaires James got in his mailbox?"

"Come on. How would she have access to my mailbox?" James said.

"Don't you work at the campus post office?" Evan asked Sloane.

For a minute the girl looked like she was going to deny it. Were we wrong? But she couldn't meet Evan's eyes. "I do," Sloane said, looking at the ground.

I was afraid I was going to be sick. Sloane was behind all the sabotage. How could anyone do such a thing?

"You'd better start explaining. Now," Evan said, facing off with her.

Sloane looked from me to James to Evan then threw up her hands. "What do you want me to say? You got me, okay? I did it. I did all of it."

"But why?" I asked. "What did we ever do to you?"

"Look, I *have* to win that automatic *A*?" Sloane said. "I'm a psych *major*, okay? And I totally tanked the midterm. If I don't ace this class, I'm never going to get the courses I want next year."

"So what? You couldn't trust that our project would be just as good as theirs or better?" Evan said. "You had to play dirty?"

Sloane's face went hard when she saw the disgusted way Evan was looking at her. "I did what I had to do," she said.

"Fine," James said. "Then we'll do what we have to do. I'm reporting this to the professor."

Go, James! I thought as he and Evan and I turned to leave. Sloane deserved to be reported.

She couldn't get away with sabotaging her peers.

"Please don't, you guys," Sloane begged, jogging to get in front of us. "He'll flunk me. You know he will."

Against my will, I felt a little sorry for her. She looked so desperate.

Evan must have noticed it, too, because he backed off. "Fine. We won't report you," he said. "But I'm not working with someone who would do something like this, Sloane. From now on you're on your own. And you'd better find a new project topic fast. It's due in a week."

"What? Evan! You can't do this to me," Sloane said as he started to walk past her.

"Sorry, Sloane. You did it to yourself," Evan said. Then he strolled off, and James and I followed, leaving Sloane devastated behind us.

Just go in there and ask him, I told myself, hovering outside Andrew Finnerman's closed door on Thursday evening. *It won't be that big a deal. It probably happens all the time.*

Trying to squelch the fear in my chest, I reached out and rapped on the door. *Here goes nothing.*

"Come in!" Andrew's voice called out.

I opened the door and stuck my head inside. "Is this a bad time?" I asked, half hoping he would tell me to come back later.

"No! Come in!" Andrew said. He pushed a key on his computer and stood up. "You have my article for me?" he asked, glancing at my hands. I swallowed a huge lump in my throat. "You don't have an article for me," he said.

"Actually, I was kind of hoping for an extension," I said in a rush.

Andrew hung his head. He reached up and pinched the bridge of his nose between his thumb and forefinger. Then he sighed. "An extension?"

"Just a day or two," I said, though I had no idea how I would finish the article in a day or two. I hadn't even started it yet.

Andrew sat down again. "I knew I shouldn't have given this to a high schooler," he muttered.

Suddenly all the blood rushed to my head. "Wait a minute. What's that supposed to mean?"

"Just that someone with no experience is never going to be able to do a piece on the prankster," Andrew said flatly, looking me in the eye.

"I didn't say I wasn't going to get the story. I just asked for a small extension!" I exclaimed.

"Oh, so you have the story?" he asked, eyebrows raised.

"I do. Or . . . I will," I told him. "I have a couple of good sources. I just . . . have to pin them down. This isn't a topic people are all that willing to talk about, you know. It takes a little time."

Andrew narrowed his eyes at me as if he was trying to decide whether he could still trust me. I wasn't totally sure he should, but I wanted him to anyway. I didn't want to be a failure.

Finally he sighed again. "Fine," he said, reaching for his mouse. "But I need the copy by tomorrow if it's going to make it into Monday's issue. Tomorrow. No ifs, ands, or buts. Got it?"

"Got it," I said, putting my hands up in surrender. "You'll have your article tomorrow. I promise."

"Good," Andrew said, glancing up at me. "You'd better go get to work then."

"Right," I said, my heart jumping. "I'm off. To get to work."

I smiled at him quickly, then slipped out of his office, closing the door behind me. Outside, I let out a long sigh and leaned back against the door. All around me reporters chatted on the phone, questioned their sources, and typed into their computers so fast that their fingers were a blur. I would have given anything to be one of them—to be writing up my story right now instead of dreading my next move.

My next move, I thought, edging away from the door. *I have to make my next move, and I have to do it soon.*

Unfortunately, I had no idea what my next move was going to be.

chapter eleven

"Well, that was a complete waste of time," I muttered to myself as I walked out of Crosby Hall.

I had finally pinned down John Francine and gotten an interview, but he had no new information. The day the prankster had struck, he had ducked into the locker room during a game, taken his mascot head off to cool down, and gone for a cold drink. When he came back, the armadillo head was gone, and a huge pig head had been left in its place. No one had seen anyone suspicious lurking around and John had missed the second half of the game. The next day, when he came in for practice, his armadillo head had been returned to the costume closet. The campus police had decided not to investigate the theft because the head wasn't damaged, and that was that.

I had asked John every question I could think of. Did he have any enemies? Did anyone particularly resent the mascot? Was there someone who wanted to *be* the mascot? Maybe someone who had tried out and lost the role to him? But John had told me that as far as he knew, there was no one out there motivated to take him down. Everyone loved the UCM armadillo.

Okay, what am I going to do now? I wondered, stopping outside the post office. An impromptu touch football game was taking place on the lush grass in front of me. Somewhere in one of the dorms someone was blasting dance music. Everyone seemed to be doing something relaxing or fun except me. I leaned back against the wall and sighed. I needed a lead, and I needed one now.

Then something across the square caught my eye. A guy walking into Marshall Hall, the dorm across the way. A tall, thin, brown-haired guy. Suddenly I was on full alert.

"Omigosh! That's him!" I gasped. "You! Hey, you! Pledge boy!" I shouted, racing across the green. "Hey! Stop!"

The shouts and cheers of the football players must have drowned out my voice. As I cut right through the center of their game, the pledge opened the door to the dorm and disappeared inside.

"Hey! You're pretty good! Wanna play running back?" one of the guys called after me.

"Not right now, thanks!" I shouted back.

I pounded on the glass door to Marshall Hall until the security guard finally came over and pushed it open. He looked tired and exasperated.

"Thank you so much!" I said. "I know you can't let me in without a key and all, but this guy just went inside, and I have to talk to him."

"Sorry. We're not in the habit of letting stalkers into our dorms," he said with a smirk.

"No! It's not like that!" I said desperately. "I'm a reporter for the *UCM Herald* and I need to interview him for a story."

The man looked me up and down, his blue eyes hard, and sighed. "What's this kid's name?"

I gulped. "I . . . don't know."

"Yeah. Nice try," the guard said, backing away.

"Wait! I don't know because he's anonymous!" I wailed.

"If he's so 'anonymous' then why do you know where he lives?" the guy asked.

"Because I met him once and I just saw him go inside." My frustration was growing. I was *so* close.

"Well, if you met him once, then you know his name, and you can call him from the security phone," the guard said. "Have a nice night."

Then he closed the door on me. Why did the people around here have to be so unhelpful? I groaned and walked to the security phone. Just staring at the useless yellow box made me so frustrated, I kicked the wall beneath it. The pain was mind-bending.

"Ow!" I shouted, gripping my toe. *Mental note: Do not let frustration make you kick stuff. Especially not brick walls.*

I hopped to a bench at the side of the building and sat down, massaging my foot. There was only one thing I could do—sit here until the pledge came out again. He would have to leave the dorm eventually, right? For a class or dinner or to hang with his friends. And when he did, I would be here. It was my only hope.

I stood outside the on-campus movie theater that night, my feet aching. James and I had spent the entire evening hitting all the most romantic spots on campus, trying to scare up a few more couples for our test group. James stood a couple yards away, interviewing a pair of grad students, while I watched the crowd pouring out of the last showing.

A guy and girl, fingers entwined, walked toward me. I automatically stepped up to them and smiled. "Hi! Would you two like to participate in our couples' survey?" I asked brightly.

"Thanks anyway," the guy said, pulling his girlfriend away.

My face fell, and I turned to the next pair I saw—an older couple who were clearly professors.

"Hi! Would you two like to participate in our couples' survey?" I asked.

"Actually, this is just our first date," the woman said, her cheeks growing pink. "I don't think we qualify as a couple."

"But good luck!" the man said before they walked off.

"You, too," I muttered, watching them join hands.

"How's it going?" James asked, coming over to me.

"Not so well," I admitted. "I'm so tired I think I've lost my touch. No one wants to talk to me."

"Well, no one has to," James said. "That couple I just finished with gives us fifty pairs."

"You're kidding!" I said, my eyes widening. "That was our goal."

"Yep," James said triumphantly. "We have enough to really start on our paper."

"James! You're the best!" I exclaimed, giving him a huge hug.

"Hey, you did as much work tonight as I did," he said.

"True. I did start off strong," I replied proudly, thinking of the seven couples I had interviewed in our first hour at the coffee shop.

"So, want to head over to the library and get started on the writing?" James asked.

I looked off toward the hulking structure of the library. The very thought of finding a table, firing up my computer, and trying to concentrate made my whole body cry out for my bed.

"Or maybe not," James said. "You look so exhausted."

"It's that obvious?" I said with a small laugh. "Actually I just don't think I'd be much help right now. I can barely see straight, let alone think straight."

"Okay, how about we go home, get a good night's sleep, and get together to work tomorrow?" James suggested, stuffing his notebook and pen into his bag.

"You know, I really lucked out getting you as a partner," I said.

"And I lucked out getting you," he said. "We are so going to ace this paper."

"Sloane had no idea who she was dealing with," I added happily.

James grinned. "You got that right."

I sat at the computer in Ashley's bedroom, typing as fast as my fingers could peck keys. After sitting outside Marshall Hall for two hours I had been forced to give up the waiting game. The pledge was never coming out. At least not before I had to meet Ashley to drive home.

Who is the UCM Prankster? I typed. *Thanks to his cunning and stealth, we may never know.*

I sat back in Ashley's desk chair and sighed. "And thanks to *me*," I muttered. "and my total lack of reporter's skills, we may never know."

"Hey. How's it going?" Ashley asked, trudging in from the bathroom. She looked like she could fall asleep right where she was standing.

"Not so good," I admitted. "I'm doing a rundown of all the prankster's pranks so far. It's about all I can do right now."

"Well, don't worry. You're a good writer," Ashley said, patting me on the shoulder and yawning as she walked by. "I'm sure it'll be ten times funnier and more insightful than anything the paper has run before."

She sank down onto her bed and folded the covers over her legs from the side, as if she was too tired even to pull down the sheets.

"Are you okay?" I asked.

"I have never been so overwhelmed in my life," Ashley said, closing her eyes. "James and I spent three hours interviewing people today. We've done all this work, and we haven't even *started* writing the paper yet."

"Wow," I said.

"Tell me about it," Ashley replied. "And this is just one class. Imagine if I had four classes like this."

If Ashley was this wiped out from taking one three-credit class for a few weeks, how did anyone find the energy to take a full course load and do extracurriculars? Like writing for the paper. Was I ever going to be able to handle being a college reporter?

So far it doesn't seem like it, I thought morosely.

"I think I have the first line for my project for Ms. Hahn," I announced.

"Oh, yeah?" Ashley asked, hugging her pillow as she yawned again. "What's that?"

"Well, the assignment is, 'What's college really like?' right?" I said.

"Oh! I know this one!" Ashley said, lifting her head slightly.

"College is hard!" we said at the same time.

Ashley laughed, and her head hit the pillow again. I saved my work and turned off the computer so my sister could get some sleep. I would have to finish my story downstairs. Maybe I would even make some coffee on my way.

There's one more thing I can add to my paper for Ms. Hahn and the story for the school Web site, I thought, glancing at my dozing sister. *I now understand why college kids consume so much caffeine.*

chapter twelve

On Friday afternoon I sat at the desk I had claimed in the *Herald* office, my left leg bouncing up and down with nerves. I couldn't stop staring at the door to Andrew's office. He had been in there reading my piece for the last ten minutes. Waiting for him to come out was like waiting at the dentist's office while he studied my X-rays and decided whether or not I had any cavities to fill.

"You all right over there?" Shelby asked.

"Uh . . . yeah," I replied, never taking my eyes off the door.

"Don't worry. Andrew's a good editor. He's tough but fair," Shelby said. "You'll be fine."

I was just starting to relax at these words when the door suddenly opened and Andrew stuck his head out. He did not look pleased.

"Olsen? Can I see you?" he said.

I stood and shot Shelby a worried look. Shelby

smiled confidently back, but my knees were quaking as I picked up my backpack and slipped past Andrew into his office. He closed the door with a bang. Was he angry, or was I just so sensitive that the sound seemed louder than it was?

"Well, I have to tell you, I'm very disappointed," Andrew said, sitting down behind his desk.

Wow. This guy definitely doesn't pull any punches, I thought, my heart sinking to stomach level. I dropped into the chair across from him.

"Look, I wasn't expecting a miracle," Andrew continued, folding his hands over my article, which was covered with red marks. "No one on my staff has figured out who the prankster is, so I had no reason to believe you would do any better. I just wanted you to shoot for the stars, and I hoped for the best. But I expected more than a report summing up all the articles we've already run."

"I'm sorry," I said, at a loss. "I tried."

"Did you really think I was going to be able to print this?" he asked.

"Well, no. I guess not," I replied, flushing.

"Then why even give it to me?" Andrew asked.

"I had to give you something," I said. "I was up all night working on that. You have no idea how hard it is."

I bit my bottom lip, suddenly realizing how whiny I sounded. I was overtired, overstressed, and feeling down about my reporting skills. But I shouldn't be letting that show in front of my editor. I was supposed to be professional.

Andrew leaned back and looked at me sympathetically. "How hard what is?" he asked gently.

"Everything," I said with a sigh. "There's all this college lingo I don't get. I did have a source, but he kept asking to meet me in places I'd never even heard of. Like what are the tombs, anyway?"

"The tombs? That's what we call the basement of the library where they keep all the old history books and stuff," Andrew said.

"See? I didn't know that! And I couldn't ask anybody without looking like a moron!" I exclaimed. "And then there are about five Crosby buildings and three 'centers,' and the security at the dorms is better than at Fort Knox. Plus do you have any idea how *huge* this place is?"

Once I started, it was as if I couldn't stop.

"And on top of all the work for this piece, I have the project that got me here in the first place, plus I'm writing a piece for the school Web site about what it's like to be in college," I said. "I'm losing my mind over here."

I took a deep breath. It felt good to finally let out all my frustrations. Andrew leaned forward, resting his elbows on the desk, and stared at me. Oh, God. He was going to call me a huge baby.

Either that or throw me out of his office for being totally incompetent.

"A piece for your high school Web site on what it's like to be in college?" he asked, raising his eyebrows. "Do you have that with you?"

I blinked, surprised. "Yeah, actually," I said, unzipping my backpack. "It's just a first draft, though."

I pulled out the article and passed it to him. Andrew's eyes darted over the page. As he read, he started to smile. Then he sat back again and chuckled. Okay, was he laughing *at* my writing because it was so bad, or was he loving my jokes?

"See, now this is a piece I could run with," he said finally, putting down the article.

My mouth dropped open. "That? But I was basically just venting."

"And your voice totally comes through. A good, strong, funny voice," Andrew said.

A warm feeling sprouted in my chest. He *did* like my writing. I *was* talented!

"I'd like to make you a deal," Andrew said. "I'll run this piece tomorrow and give you another few days to track down the prankster. But this time, when you're stuck, I expect you to ask for help, okay? There's nothing wrong with asking for a little help."

"Got it," I said with a nod. Suddenly I was

more determined than ever to write the prankster article. "I won't let you down this time, Andrew."

We both stood and Andrew stuck out his hand. "So we have a deal?" he asked.

I grinned and shook on it with him. "Deal." I turned and opened the door but paused before walking out. "And, Andrew," I said over my shoulder, "thanks for the second chance."

"We're never going to get there in time!" I shouted as James and I ran toward our psychology professor's office.

"Your watch is fast! We have five minutes until the deadline!" James replied, jumping down a set of stairs.

I yanked open the door at the bottom of the stairwell, and James sprinted through, clutching our twenty-page paper—our baby. We had just finished printing it at the computer center ten minutes ago, and our professor was only taking papers until five o'clock. It was crunch time.

James ran to the office and skidded to a stop. The door was ajar and I could hear voices inside.

"But, Professor, it's not my fault my partner dropped me just before the project was due."

I recognized that voice. "Sloane?" I whispered.

James nodded and tried to control his breathing. We were both sucking wind after our sprint.

"Actually, Sloane, from all my experience teaching, it can *only* be your fault you were dropped," the professor said. "I'm sorry, but I have no choice but to give you an *F* on your final project."

"But, Professor . . ." Sloane tried again, her voice cracking.

Again I felt sorry for the girl.

"If you'll excuse me, I seem to have someone waiting for me outside," the professor said quietly.

Suddenly the door was flung open all the way and Sloane barged out. She took one look at me, and the color drained from her face.

"This is all your fault," she said.

"*My* fault? *You* tried to sabotage *our* project," I replied.

"Yeah, but Evan never would have cared if he wasn't going out with you," Sloane said. "I'm going to have to retake this class, thanks to you."

"Well, better luck next time," James said evenly.

"Watch your back, Ashley," Sloane warned, narrowing her eyes at me and ignoring James.

Sloane stormed off, and I just stood there for a moment, shocked. What was wrong with that girl?

"Ignore her," James said. "Let's hand in our project."

As James and I talked with the professor, all I could think about was how much information I had for Ms. Hahn. I had learned a lot about college. Work hard, be prepared for anything, and keep your laptop away from psychos like Sloane.

"Well, I think we need a burger to celebrate," James said as we walked out of the building.

"I couldn't agree more," I replied. Now that the stress of completing the paper was over, I was starving.

As we cut across campus, enjoying the high of having handed in our project, I noticed a crowd of people clamoring around Marshall Hall, one of the freshman dorms.

"What's going on?" I asked.

"Beats me," James said. "Let's find out."

As we walked over, I spotted Mary-Kate on the outskirts of the crowd. "Hey! There's my sister!"

"You have a sister?" James asked.

"I didn't mention that?" I asked. "Wow. I guess we really *have* been working hard!"

We jogged the last few steps toward the crowd.

"Hey, Mary-Kate!" I called out. "What's up?"

Mary-Kate turned to me, her eyes bright with excitement. "It's the prankster! He's struck again! He caulked every bathroom door in the dorm shut so that no one could get in to them!"

"And you're excited because . . . ?" I inquired.

"I'm not excited about the *prank*, Ashley," Mary-Kate said, gripping my arms. "I'm excited because I finally have a real lead!"

chapter thirteen

"**I** think my informant is actually the prankster," I told Ashley and James as we all grabbed a table at Jimmy's, a burger shop on campus. "I think it's driving him crazy that he can't take credit for his brilliance. I think he wants to confess."

"Hold on. That doesn't make any sense," Ashley said, taking a sip of her soda.

"Gee, thanks, sis," I said flatly.

"I hate to say it, but Ashley's got a point," James put in. "If he wanted to confess, why didn't he just tell you the first time you met him?"

"Because he couldn't tell me in front of all his fraternity brothers," I said with a shrug.

"Okay, let's backtrack," Ashley said, grabbing a fry to munch on. "What's your evidence?"

A thrill of excitement rushed up my spine. I was so proud of myself for figuring this out.

"Well, he totally dropped the ball with this last

prank," I explained. "See, the informant lives in Marshall Hall, and you can't get into any of the dorms unless you have an ID and a key for that specific dorm. So only a person who lives there could have caulked all the bathrooms shut."

I grinned, but Ashley and James just stared at me blankly.

"What?" I asked, shaking some ketchup onto my burger.

"Well, anyone who lives in Marshall could have signed the guy in," James said. "He could still be anybody."

"I thought of that," I said. "The bathrooms were caulked first thing this morning, so I talked to the security guard on duty. No one signed in that early and everyone who signed in last night signed out before the prank happened."

"Interesting," Ashley said, starting to jump on board. "So what's your next move?"

"Well, I've got to get a list of all the guys who live in Marshall Hall," I said. "Then I just have to find out which of those guys has access to the cafeteria—"

"Because of the green eggs," James finished.

"The coffee house, because of the iced-tea trick," Ashley added.

"Right. And maybe someone who would have a grudge against the basketball team," I finished.

"Since he painted the bus pink and stole the mascot's head."

"Wow," James said. "You've really thought of everything."

"I think I have," I said happily. "I just wish I had a picture of the pledge to show around. I can describe him, but he's pretty normal looking. Tall, brown hair, brown eyes. He could be anyone."

We pondered this for a while, but then James had to leave for a study group.

"A picture," Ashley said thoughtfully after James left. "What about the yearbook?"

"He's a freshman, and it won't come out until the spring," I said. "Besides, there would be hundreds and hundreds of photos to look through." I took a deep breath and popped a French fry into my mouth. "If only I could get into the Squash house again. . . ."

Ashley sat up a little straighter. "Sigma Kappa Zeta? Why do you want to get in there?"

"He's pledging there," I explained. "They must have a picture of him somewhere."

"That's perfect! *I* can get you into the Squash house," Ashley said.

My heart skipped a beat. "You can? How!?"

"Sigma Kappa Zeta is Evan's fraternity," Ashley replied.

"Omigosh! You're the best sister ever!" I cried,

leaning over all the food to hug Ashley. "Except . . . how come I haven't learned this before now?"

Ashley laughed. "I guess the psychology project fried my brain," she said with a casual shrug and a smile. "But just don't say I never helped with your career."

❀

"Hey!" I said when Evan opened his door. "We just thought we'd drop by and say hello."

Evan grinned and stepped back so Mary-Kate and I could get by. "This is a nice surprise," he said. "Sorry about the mess. If I'd known you were coming, I would have cleaned up."

I glanced around the room, taking in the pile of clothes on the floor, the messy bed, and the open pizza box on the desk.

"Not a problem," I told him. I noticed a stack of pictures next to the pizza on his desk and picked them up. "Are these the pictures of your friends?" I asked casually. I saw Mary-Kate's eyes light up, and she stepped behind me to look over my shoulder.

"Yeah," Evan said. "I was telling Ashley how I'm in charge of putting together the brotherhood photo album this year, so everybody has to give me pictures."

"Cool," Mary-Kate said. "Mind if we look?"

"Knock yourselves out," Evan replied, taking

the pizza box and heading for the door. "I'm just going to go toss this. Be right back."

"We'll be here!" I replied.

"This is so perfect!" Mary-Kate whispered as I flipped quickly through the photos.

"Stop me if you see the pledge," I told her.

There were pictures of a bunch of guys at an outdoor barbecue, then a bunch of pictures of kids in pledge T-shirts doing gardening in the backyard.

"There he is!" Mary-Kate said, grabbing a photo of two guys grinning at the camera with shovels in their hands. "This is my informant!"

"Hey, do you two want anything to drink?" Evan asked, walking back in.

"No thanks," Mary-Kate said, turning to him. "Do you know this guy?" she asked, pointing at her informant in the picture.

"Know him? Sure. That's Mitchell Krantz," Evan said. "He's pledging right now. Cool kid. He's totally hilarious," he added with a chuckle.

Mary-Kate grinned at me. *Hilarious, huh?* I thought. *Kind of like the prankster?*

"May I borrow this picture?" Mary-Kate asked, breathless.

I hadn't seen my sister this excited since the huge mall-wide sale last summer.

"Uh, sure," Evan said. "I don't see why not."

"Thanks! Gotta go!" Mary-Kate said. Then she

hugged me quickly and bolted. "I'll call you on your cell!" she shouted over her shoulder.

"Go get 'im!" I called after her, excited.

Evan looked at me, confused.

"Don't mind my sister," I said with a laugh, trying to cover our suspicious behavior. "She's just a little . . . hyper."

Evan smiled. "Ah. I know the type," he said, sitting down at his desk.

"What do you mean?" I asked.

"That ex I told you about? She was flighty and all over the place like that," Evan replied, lifting one shoulder. "But what do you expect? She was in high school."

I felt as if I had been slapped. There it was again—the anti–high school prejudice. "So . . . what?" I said. "All high school girls are immature?"

"No. Of course not," Evan said. "I just wouldn't date one again."

My stomach clenched, and I sat down on his roommate's desk chair.

"I mean, all my friends gave me a hard time about it because I had to leave campus to see her, and she couldn't come to any of our parties," he said. "It was a total hassle."

Suddenly I felt nauseated. I really liked Evan. A lot. But would he still like me if he knew who I really was?

chapter fourteen

Saturday morning I stood in the cafeteria kitchen as workers in hairnets prepared huge vats of scrambled eggs and hundreds of strips of bacon.

A large man in a white uniform walked out from the back room with the girl I had spoken to when I first arrived.

"I'm Mr. Ronald, the manager," he said. "You wanted to see me?"

"Hi. I just have a quick question," I said, taking out my photo of the Squash pledge. "Do you know this guy?"

"Sure. Mitchell Krantz," Mr. Ronald said, glancing down at the photo. "He's one of my best workers."

I grinned. Score! "When is his next shift?"

"He's working dinner tonight," Mr. Ronald said. Then he narrowed his eyes. "Why?"

"Just have something I need to ask him," I

said, turning to move on to my next destination. "Thanks!"

"Yeah, I know Mitchell Krantz," the pink-haired girl at Cuppa Joe told me, popping her gum. "He's going out with our assistant manager, Casey."

"Really?" I asked. I could barely contain a triumphant grin. "So would you say he's here a lot?"

"Oh, all the time," the girl replied. "He practically lives here. Sometimes he and Casey even eat lunch in the stockroom together."

"Thanks," I said, pocketing the photo once more. "That's all I needed to know."

Access to the cafeteria, check. Access to Cuppa Joe's stockroom, check, I thought. *Just one more meeting, and I'll know I've got my man.*

"Mitchell Krantz is a good kid," Coach Wyatt said, kicking back in his chair at the athletic offices. "It was too bad I had to fire him."

"Fire him?" I asked, intrigued.

"Yep. Mitchell was the team's equipment manager until about a month ago," Coach Wyatt said. "Then he started pledging that fraternity of his."

"What happened then?" I asked.

"He was always late and half asleep most of the time," Wyatt replied. "Couldn't do the job anymore, so I had to let him go."

"How did he take it?" I asked, leaning forward.

"Not well," Wyatt said, lifting his red baseball cap to scratch an itch on his forehead. "He argued with me for an hour. Really enjoyed traveling with the team and all that. He was still very upset when he left."

Upset with the coach of the basketball team? That was all I needed to hear.

"Well, thanks for your time," I said, standing. I was so excited, my hands were actually shaking. I had my man. Mitchell Krantz was obviously the campus prankster.

On Saturday evening I stood in front of my full-length mirror and smoothed the skirt of my favorite red dress. I looked at my reflection and sighed. My hair was up in a curly ponytail with wisps hanging around my face. My makeup was just right—subtle but sophisticated—perfect for my first college dance. But for some reason I just wasn't excited.

"Hey! You look amazing!" Mary-Kate said, standing at the door. Then her brow furrowed, and she frowned. "Why so miserable?"

"It's Evan," I admitted, my shoulders slumping.

"Evan? What's wrong with Evan?" Mary-Kate asked. "He's such a great guy, and he's so . . . well . . . the word *charming* comes to mind."

"I know," I said, trying to smile. I sat on my bed and looked down at my hands. "It's just, I think that if he knew I was in high school, I wouldn't even be going to this dance tonight."

"What do you mean?" Mary-Kate asked, sitting down next to me.

"He and his friends are always saying they think high school girls are silly and immature," I confessed. "And just yesterday he told me that he wouldn't want to go out with anyone who didn't live on campus. He said it was too much of a pain."

"Whoa," Mary-Kate said. "That's harsh."

"I know. But I like him so much," I said, my heart turning over. "What if he finds out who I really am and doesn't want me around?"

"First, anyone who wouldn't want you around is an idiot," Mary-Kate said. "Second, I hate seeing you like this."

"I know. I hate feeling like this," I said. "I just feel so . . . uncertain."

"You need to tell Evan that you're really in high school," Mary-Kate said. "If he doesn't want to be with you, then he's not worth it anyway."

I let her words sink in and sat up a little straighter. I had been thinking the same thing all day, but hearing Mary-Kate say it made me feel all the more sure that it was the right thing to do. "You're right. I'm going to tell Evan who I really am. And then we'll find out who *he* really is."

"Good for you," Mary-Kate said, throwing her arms around me. "You nervous?"

"Totally," I said with a laugh. "But it's going to be fine. I'm going to talk to him tonight. Thanks, Mary-Kate."

"Hey," Mary-Kate said with a shrug. "It's what I do."

An hour later, while Ashley was across campus at the Sigma Kappa Zeta dance, I stood outside the back door of the cafeteria and waited. Any minute now Mitchell Krantz would get off work. Any minute now I would finally have my story.

The door flew open, and Mitchell stepped out, head down, looking tired after a long shift of work. This was it. I stepped from the shadows, my heart pounding with anticipation, and Mitchell paused.

"Still want to talk?" I asked.

"I already gave you a couple of chances, and you didn't show," he said, walking right by me.

Don't let him go! a panicked voice in my mind shouted.

"Come on, Mitchell," I said. "Or should I call you . . . the prankster?"

Mitchell stopped in his tracks. I had him! Victory was *so* sweet! Slowly he turned around and looked me in the eye.

"I never said I was the prankster," he said. "I told you I *know* who the prankster is."

For a split second I was at a loss for words. He was denying it. Was it possible that I had been wrong all along? But no. I had done my legwork this time. I had my evidence. He was just trying to mess with me. I had to stay strong.

"Look, Mitchell, I've asked around about you," I said. "You work at the cafeteria, so you have access to the food. You could have snagged your boss's universal key to get into the janitors' closets and the dean's garage. Your girlfriend works at Cuppa Joe. You have a grudge against the basketball team. *And* you live in Marshall Hall. It all leads back to you."

Mitchell smiled slowly and shook his head. "You think you've got it all figured out, don't you?"

"Yeah, I kind of think I do," I said confidently, crossing my arms over my chest.

"Well, you're really warm, but I think I'll let you figure out the rest on your own." He turned to walk away again and my heart plummeted.

"Wait!" I called after him, desperate to keep my one lead from getting away again. "If you're not the prankster, then who is? You were going to tell me before, so tell me now!"

"Talk to your friends at the fraternity!" Mitchell shouted, turning to walk backward. "One of them might be very helpful!"

chapter fifteen

"Hello! Anybody home?" I shouted as I pounded on the door of the Squash house. I knew they were holding a dance in the gym that night, but maybe someone was there. Finally the door opened, and a guy with spiked red hair stood there in a pledge T-shirt, looking confused.

"Hi!" I said with a smile. "Is Evan still here?"

"Nope. He left for the dance already," the guy said.

"Okay, what about . . . Darnell? Or . . . or Stan?" I asked, racking my brain for names.

"Darnell is out, and Stan is at the dance, too," the kid said. "Sorry."

He started to close the door, but I could not get shut out again. "David?" I said, blurting the first common name that came to mind. "Is David here?"

The kid stopped and nodded. "He's around here somewhere. Come on in."

Thank you, thank you, thank you! I thought, stepping inside. I had no idea what I was going to do with most of the brothers gone, but at least I had gotten in. That was half the battle.

"I'll go get him for you," the pledge said.

The second he was gone, I slipped upstairs. If I could just check a couple of the rooms—see if I spotted anything suspicious—maybe I could narrow down my suspects. After Mitchell's little clue, I was more certain than ever that one of the Sigma Kappa Zeta brothers was the prankster.

Down the hall a door closed, and my heart hit my throat. Panicking, I grabbed the nearest doorknob. The white message board on the door read: *Darnell! Meet me at Econ! Rob.* It was Darnell's room. I slipped inside and closed the door behind me. Outside, a couple of guys walked down the hall, talking about their plans for Christmas break. I took a deep breath and looked around.

Darnell had wallpapered his room with basketball paraphernalia. Posters of classic players like Michael Jordan and Magic Johnson hung next to pictures of the current Lakers team and U.S. Olympics teams. But the wall next to his bed was like a shrine to Darnell himself. Framed newspaper articles shouted headlines such as: *Darnell Does It Again!* and *Darnell White Breaks County Scoring Record!* There were pictures of Darnell, grinning at the camera, clutching various trophies.

"Wow. Major b-ball star," I whispered. I turned to check out his desk, and my heart thumped. Right on the edge was a framed photo of Darnell with his arm around Mitchell Krantz. The etching in the wooden frame read: *Big Bro, Little Bro.*

So Darnell and Mitchell are close, I thought, my pulse racing. *This has to mean something, but what?*

A voice in the hall startled me, and I turned and jammed my toe on something that was sticking out from under the bed.

"Ouch!" I whispered, bending to inspect the object. It was a big black photo album. My reporter's instincts kicked in. I grabbed the album, sat on the bed, and flipped it open.

Taped to the first page was an article from the *UCM Herald.* The headline, over a grinning picture of Darnell, read: *Top Basketball Prospect to Attend Malibu.* The next article outlined a major scholarship for Darnell. But the next talked about his failures on the court, and the next blamed a huge loss on the disappointing freshman. Finally there was article about Darnell, once a rising star, getting cut from the team.

"He totally choked," I said. "How awful."

I turned the page, and time seemed to stop. It was the first article about the prankster—the one about the stolen benches. On the next page was the article about the dean's license plates. My throat going dry, I flipped through the book all the way to the end. Every single prankster article had been carefully clipped and laid out.

No one but the prankster himself would have taken the time to do something like this. Could it be? Was Darnell White the campus prankster?

Omigosh, it makes perfect sense, I thought. Darnell had a much bigger grudge against the basketball team than Mitchell did, and he and Mitchell were close. Mitchell must have helped him get into all those places that only *he* had access to. Mitchell wasn't the prankster. He was just an accomplice!

Suddenly the door to the bedroom opened. I had no time to hide. When Darnell stepped into his room, I was sitting there on his bed, his scrapbook open on my lap.

Darnell looked at me, looked at the album, and froze. "What are you doing in here?"

I swallowed hard. I had been caught red-handed snooping around someone's room. All I could do was hope that Darnell would appreciate someone almost as sneaky as him.

"I've always wanted to meet the prankster," I said steadily.

Darnell blinked, and for a second I thought he

was going to yell at me, but instead he smiled. A huge, wide smile.

"Well," he said. "It's about time someone figured it out."

❈

"Have I told you how beautiful you look tonight?" Evan asked as he led me onto the dance floor that night.

"Only five times," I said with a smile.

"Well, there's always room for one more," Evan said.

I grinned and stepped closer to him as we moved to the music. So far the evening was perfect. Evan looked gorgeous in his suit and tie. The dance was being held in the same gym the Black Tombs had performed in, but the place had been transformed into a winter wonderland. White lights twinkled everywhere. Paper snowflakes hung from silver and white strings attached to gleaming helium balloons. There were Christmas trees in every corner, and one of the brothers had dressed up as Santa. He was seated at the back of the room, hearing everyone's Christmas wishes.

Maybe I should wait until the end of the night to tell Evan, I thought. I didn't want to spoil the whole evening with a serious talk. All I wanted to do was keep dancing.

"May I cut in?"

I looked up to find Sloane standing beside us in a blue gown, her hands on her hips and a nasty smirk on her face. Clutched in her fingers was a copy of the *UCM Herald*.

"What are you doing here?" Evan asked.

"I just think it's interesting that you can't finish a project with me because I'm so dishonest, but you can dance with someone who's even worse," Sloane said.

My heart skipped a scared beat, and Evan looked down at me, confused.

"What's she talking about?" he asked.

"I . . . I don't know," I said. There was no way Sloane could have found out I didn't go to Malibu, was there?

"I'm talking about this," Sloane said, thrusting the paper forward. She opened it to the second page, and my stomach twisted into a knot. Mary-Kate's school picture was printed under the headline, *High Schooler Poses as College Student.*

"This is your sister," Evan said, grabbing the paper. He looked totally stunned. "Your *twin* sister. You guys are in high school?"

I felt as if someone had yanked the floor out from under me. His exclamation drew a little crowd, including Stan and his date. They all bent over the paper and passed it around, snickering and smirking.

"Yes. We are," I said, glancing at Sloane's triumphant expression. "I was going to tell you tonight. I'm sorry I lied, but it was all part of this school project."

"Wow. Nice work, Ev. Duped by a high school kid," Stan said. "I knew she reminded me of Giggle Fit."

My mouth dropped open. "I thought you said I was so much cooler than Giggle Fit," I pointed out. "Amazing how quickly your opinion changes."

"Ooh! Uh-oh! Is the baby going to cry?" Stan teased.

My face flushed bright red, and I turned to Evan. It didn't matter what Stan thought of me. Evan was the only one I cared about. "Can we talk about this, please?"

"No, we can't," he said, his face hard. "I'm sorry, Ashley, but I don't date girls in high school. Not anymore."

He turned and pushed through the crowd, heading for the door. I was so shocked. I couldn't move. He wasn't even going to let me explain. How could someone who had seemed so sweet and cool turn out to be such a jerk? Mary-Kate was right. Evan was not worth another moment of my time.

"Told you to watch your back," Sloane said, handing me the newspaper. Then she scurried off after Evan. The rest of the guys broke away, hiding their smiles behind their hands. I only wished they could see how immature they looked while they were picking on *me* for being young.

Well, no reason to stick around here, I thought, turning to go and walking right into James. He was out of breath and grinning from ear to ear.

"Ashley! I thought you'd be here," he said.

"James! What's going on?" I asked.

"I just stopped by Professor Alexander's office to see if he had left out the graded projects in the box on his door yet and he had," James said.

My heart skipped a beat. "What did we get?"

James whipped our folded paper from his back pocket. There was a big red *A* on the top.

"I don't believe it!" I cried. "I got an *A* in a college-level class!"

"College level?" James said.

"Oh, you missed the big scandal?" I said, no longer caring who knew my secret. I was too psyched to care. "I'm actually in high school."

James blinked, then grinned. "Yeah, I know."

"What?" I asked, holding my breath. How did he know?

"When the project was assigned we had to register our partners with the professor, remember?" James started to explain. "Well, when I gave him our names, he told me you were here as part of a special project for your high school. He asked me if I minded working with you."

"And you didn't?" I stared at James in total amazement.

"Of course not. I took one look at how furiously you took notes during the lecture and I knew I was safe with you." James smiled. "It totally paid off. I haven't told you the best part yet."

"You're killing me here . . ." I said anxiously.

"Ashley, we didn't just get an *A*," James said, waving a handwritten note with the psych department's name at the top. "Our project was judged best in the class. We got . . . I mean, I guess *I* got the automatic *A*!"

"Omigosh!" I said, throwing my arms around James's neck. "I'm so happy for you!"

"Happy for us," James said, releasing me. "Even though I've known the whole time, I still can't believe you're in high school. When you get to college, watch out, world."

I beamed with pride. "Thanks, James."

"So, partner, want to dance?" James asked, holding out his hand.

"I'd love to, partner," I said, slipping my fingers into his.

"And just so you know, it's pretty obvious you don't go to school here," he said as we began to dance.

"Why's that?" I asked.

"You're way too special to be just another UCM girl," he said.

Then before I could even respond, he comically dipped me backward and the whole world went upside down. I laughed as he pulled me up again and we spun across the floor, me in my beautiful dress, James in his jeans. As we danced, I realized that I might have lost an immature frat boy that night, but I had gained an amazing friend.

"I still can't believe it," Ashley said as we sat on a bench on the green on Tuesday afternoon. "My sister did what no college reporter was able to do."

"Yeah, I pretty much rock, don't I?" I said giddily. I looked down at the headline on the *UCM Herald* and grinned. *High School Reporter Nabs Prankster*. Everyone on campus was talking about the article. I was practically as famous as Darnell.

"I'm so sorry about Saturday, though, Ashley," I said, laying the paper aside. "I didn't think Andrew was going to run that article until Monday. Who knew he could get it into the weekend edition so fast?"

"It's all good," Ashley said. "It worked out for the best." She lifted the paper again and scanned the article, which took up the entire first page. "I still can't believe this Mitchell guy helped Darnell get into all those places. Wasn't he afraid he's get into trouble?"

"Well, apparently when you pledge a fraternity, you're pretty much supposed to do whatever the brothers ask you to do," I said with a shrug. "But after a while Mitchell realized that sooner or later someone might get hurt or he might get expelled. That was why he came to me."

"But they're not getting expelled, are they?" Ashley asked.

"Nope. The school tried to suspend them for a semester, but none of the students on the discipline board would agree to it," I said. "Darnell and Mitchell were only fined the cost of repainting the bus. And Andrew said a couple of the pranks made the national news. It was like free advertising, so the dean wasn't even that mad."

"College is weird," Ashley said.

"Tell me about it," I replied.

We shared a moment of silence as we both looked out across the bustling campus. I felt a thump of nostalgia in my chest as I watched the students rushing from class to class. Even though the last couple of weeks had been absolutely insane, I was actually going to miss it here. After all, I had broken my first big story at UCM, and learned that I might have what it takes to be a college reporter after all.

"So, do you think we'll make it in college?" Ashley asked.

"Definitely," I replied with a nod. "You know how to weed out the unworthy guys and the obnoxious girls—*and* how to get an *A* in class. And I now know that 'the tombs' are the basement rooms of the library, 'the center' is the Student Center, that you can't get into a dorm without ID, and that you can't get a lame story into a newspaper." I looked at Ashley with a straight face and shrugged. "It's really not that hard."

Ashley looked at me and knit her brows. "I want to go back to high school," she said.

"Me, too," I replied.

We laughed, grabbed our copies of the *Herald* and walked arm in arm across campus. College had been fun, but I knew that high school was where I really belonged.

For now.

Find out what happens next in

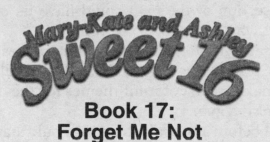

Book 17:
Forget Me Not

"You guys," I said, as my friends and I sat in the mall. "The entire junior class is counting on us to come up with a totally great theme for the Spring Fling dance. We cannot afford to screw this up. If we do, we'll have to change schools or something."

"Gee, Ashley," Melanie said. "Apply the pressure much?"

"I really hate to say this," I added. "But last year's Fling was the best ever. It's a hard act to follow, but we've got to come up with something."

"Hold everything. I am about to be brilliant," Mary-Kate suddenly announced, as her eyes grew

127

wide. "How about *Isn't It Romantic?* for a theme? Each section of the gym could have its own version of what it means to be romantic."

"That's great! It's totally what makes Spring Fling Spring Fling!" Melanie said excitedly. "Let's start making a list of mini-themes for the different parts of the gym."

But before any brainstorming could start, I saw Mary-Kate's eyes widen. She glanced at me, then cast her eyes meaningfully over my shoulder. There was clearly something behind me I ought to see.

Walking behind us was Melanie's date of last night, Anthony Martin. And he wasn't alone.

The second she saw Anthony with his arm around another girl, Melanie was going to have her heart broken.

Don't do it! Don't turn around, I thought. Too late. I knew the second she spotted Anthony. Her face went pale, and she sucked in a breath.

"We're right here with you, Melanie," Mary-Kate spoke up quickly in a low voice.

"I just don't understand it," Melanie wailed. "Why would he even go out with me if he was seeing someone else?"

"So much for *Isn't It Romantic?* I have to admit, I wasn't feeling so into the romance anyway," I remarked.

At once, the entire table looked sympathetic,

even Melanie. "Aaron?" she asked, referring to my ex-boyfriend.

I nodded. "I got a voicemail from him last night. He wants to talk. About, and I quote, something important."

"Uh-oh," Brittany muttered.

"Do you think he wants to get back together?" Lauren asked.

"I honestly don't know," I said. "And even if he does, I'm not so sure getting back together is what I want. I was really surprised to hear from him."

"How about if we just call it quits for today?" Mary-Kate suggested. "My brain is totally fried.

"Sounds good to me!" I said, grateful for my sister's solution.

Mary-Kate left for Click Café with Lauren. Brittany offered Melanie a lift. I took a moment to stroll the mall. Stopping to admire a display of hair products in a new salon, I'd spotted a reflection in the window glass.

It was Aaron, and he was heading straight toward me.

Oh, no! I thought.

Just as I was walking out of the mall with Lauren, my cell phone rang.

"Mary-Kate, it's Liam," said the voice at the other end. "Please say you remember that name."

"Liam, now let me see," I said.

"Liam McCaffrey," the voice said. "You know— from *Girlz* magazine? Liam who only owes his current career in journalism to you. Liam who also no doubt owes you a really big favor, but is hoping you'll do him one instead."

"Oh, *that* Liam!" I exclaimed.

He laughed, the sound relieved and warm.

Liam and I had worked together at *Girlz* magazine. We'd parted ways since I quit my job there.

"How are things at *Girlz*?" I asked.

"Good," Liam said. "But there is something I'd really like to talk to you about. Any chance we could meet?"

"Sure," I said, surprised. "Just say when."

"How does *now* sound?"

"Desperate," I answered with a laugh.

Liam gave a snort. "You got that in one."

"Is Click Café all right?" I asked. "I'm headed there right now."

"Perfect," Liam said. "I'll meet you there."

"Okay," I said and hung up.

"Liam—he's that guy you used to work with at *Girlz* magazine, right?" Lauren asked.

"Right," I said. "I haven't heard from him in months, now he calls and wants to meet."

"That's interesting," she said. "I wonder why."

I couldn't wait to find out.

Mary-Kate and Ashley Sweet 16
$500 Shopping Spree Sweepstakes

OFFICIAL RULES:

1. **No purchase or payment necessary to enter or win.**

2. **How to Enter.** To enter, complete the official entry form or hand print your name, address, age, and phone number along with the words *"Sweet 16* Win A Shopping Spree Sweepstakes" on a 3" x 5" card and mail to: *"Sweet 16* Win A Shopping Spree Sweepstakes" c/o HarperEntertainment, Attn: Children's Marketing Department, 10 East 53rd Street, New York, NY 10022. Entries must be received no later than June 28, 2005. Enter as often as you wish, but each entry must be mailed separately. One entry per envelope. Partially completed, illegible, or mechanically reproduced entries will not be accepted. Sponsor is not responsible for lost, late, mutilated, illegible, stolen, postage due, incomplete, or misdirected entries. All entries become the property of Dualstar Entertainment Group, LLC and will not be returned.

3. **Eligibility.** Sweepstakes open to all legal residents of the United States (excluding Colorado and Rhode Island), who are between the ages of five and fifteen on June 28, 2005 excluding employees and immediate family members of HarperCollins Publishers, Inc., ("HarperCollins"), Parachute Properties and Parachute Press, Inc., and their respective subsidiaries and affiliates, officers, directors, shareholders, employees, agents, attorneys, and other representatives and their immediate families (individually and collectively, "Parachute"), Dualstar Entertainment Group, LLC, and its subsidiaries and affiliates, officers, directors, shareholders, employees, agents, attorneys, and other representatives and their immediate families (individually and collectively, "Dualstar"), and their respective parent companies, affiliates, subsidiaries, advertising, promotion and fulfillment agencies, and the persons with whom each of the above are domiciled. All applicable federal, state and local laws and regulations apply. Offer void where prohibited or restricted by law.

4. **Odds of Winning.** Odds of winning depend on the total number of entries received. Approximately 300,000 sweepstakes announcements published. Prize will be awarded. Winner will be randomly drawn on or about July 15, 2005, by HarperCollins, whose decision is final. Potential winner will be notified by mail and will be required to sign and return an affidavit of eligibility and release of liability within 14 days of notification. Prize won by a minor will be awarded to parent or legal guardian who must sign and return all required legal documents. By acceptance of the prize, winner consents to the use of their name, photograph, likeness, and biographical information by HarperCollins, Parachute, Dualstar, and for publicity purposes without further compensation except where prohibited.

5. **Grand Prize.** One Grand Prize Winner will receive a $500 cash prize to be used at winner's discretion.

6. **Prize Limitations.** Prize will be awarded. Prize is non-transferable and cannot be sold or redeemed for cash. No cash substitute is available. Any federal, state, or local taxes are the responsibility of the winner. Sponsor may substitute prize of equal or greater value, if necessary, due to availability.

7. **Additional terms:** By participating, entrants agree a) to the official rules and decisions of the judges, which will be final in all respects; and to waive any claim to ambiguity of the official rules and b) to release, discharge, and hold harmless HarperCollins, Parachute, Dualstar, and their respective parent companies, affiliates, subsidiaries, employees and representatives and advertising, promotion and fulfillment agencies from and against any and all liability or damages associated with acceptance, use, or misuse of any prize received or participation in any Sweepstakes-related activity or participation in this Sweepstakes.

8. **Dispute Resolution.** Any dispute arising from this Sweepstakes will be determined according to the laws of the State of New York, without reference to its conflict of law principles, and the entrants consent to the personal jurisdiction of the State and Federal courts located in New York County and agree that such courts have exclusive jurisdiction over all such disputes.

9. **Winner Information.** To obtain the name of the winner, please send your request and a self-addressed stamped envelope (residents of Vermont may omit return postage) to *"Sweet 16* Win A Shopping Spree Sweepstakes" Winner, c/o HarperEntertainment, 10 East 53rd Street, New York, NY 10022 after August 15, 2005, but no later than February 15, 2006.

10. **Sweepstakes Sponsor:** HarperCollins Publishers.

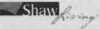

Travel the world with **Mary-Kate** and **Ashley**

www.mary-kateandashley.com

Mary-Kate Olsen   Ashley Olsen

new york minute
the movie

Experience the same hilarious trials and tribulations as Roxy and Jane did in their feature film *New York Minute*.

Bonus Movie Mini-Poster!